A REAL
AMERICAN

☆ RICHARD EASTON ☆

Clarion Books ★ New York

For my wife, Patricia, and our children,
Liz, Rick, and Matt

And for all our older family members
whose stories echo on these pages

Clarion Books
a Houghton Mifflin Company imprint
215 Park Avenue South, New York, NY 10003

The text was set in 13-point Goudy.

www.houghtonmifflinbooks.com

Printed in the USA.

ISBN: 0-618-13339-9

Full cataloging information is available from the Library of Congress.

QUM 10 9 8 7 6 5 4 3 2 1

ACKNOWLEDGMENTS

With special thanks to Michele Coppola, my editor, for her intelligent and sensitive guidance; to Dinah Stevenson, editorial director of Clarion Books, for her insightful suggestions and support; to Washington & Jefferson College librarian David Kraeuter and his staff and Peters Township librarian Pier Lee and her staff for ceaseless and enthusiastic reference assistance; to western Pennsylvania regional historian and author Helene Smith for her writings, which inspired me; to Kendra Marcus of BookStop Literary Agency for challenging me; to Leonard Marraccini, coal mine historian and federal mine safety employee, for his sound advice on coal mines and their dangers; to my W & J students and alumni, who constantly renew me; and to my weekly Pittsburgh writers group, who year after year reveal talent, values, and accomplishments that are a benchmark for me and for all who know these writers.

ONE

*N*athan McClelland looked up Robinson Road, waiting to see his last friend drive off. Like the other farm families, Ben's had sold out to the Pittsburgh coal company. Now they were moving away, too. Nathan kicked the dust with his bare foot. The *chock, chock* of axes and the shouts of the coal company men rang in his ears. Already the company was ripping down buildings on the Robinson farm.

The family's wagon, roped high with household goods, swayed into view. Ben Robinson leaped from the wagon and raced toward Nathan. Pa had said it'd be too sad to see Ben leave and the company tear apart his home, but Nathan was glad he'd come. He and Ben had been friends all their eleven years. They had even been born in the same month—January 1881. Ben didn't say a word. He just stood there, all red-faced and out of breath. Nathan stuck out his hand, and Ben shook it.

The wagon drew near. Ben's older brother, Pete, and his father, Pap Robinson, sat on the seat, stiff and sour, looking anxious to get away. At the rear of the wagon perched Ma Robinson, peering around the goods and wiping her eyes with a blue kerchief.

Nathan wanted to yell at Pap Robinson, "Why aren't you smiling? You got your cash money." Instead, he lowered his head and bit his lip.

Pap hauled the mules to a stop. Pete called out, "Look at the two namby-pambies making goodbyes. Come on, Ben. Pap wants out of here. Only numskulls would stay with all the scum moving in."

Nathan kept his head down. Why did he never have a smart comeback for bullies like Pete? Maybe because Pete was right—he and his family *were* numskulls.

Ben punched Nathan's shoulder. "Don't just stand there, McClelland. Tell him to rot. Stick up for yourself. You'll have to, now that I'll be gone."

Nathan poked Ben back and tried to smile. "Yeah, sure."

"Mount up, Ben," Pap muttered. "We ain't got all day." He flicked the reins and the wagon moved.

Backing toward it, Ben called, "The arrowheads. I dug them on the ridge. You'll see." He clambered onto the tail end of the wagon beside his ma. She waved her kerchief at Nathan.

"Hey, McClelland!" Pete hollered. "You may not think it's so bad now, with school just out, but wait till September. You'll be going to school with a bunch of stinking foreigners."

Nathan blinked and looked at Ben. "I almost forgot." He jammed his hand in the pocket of his overalls, pulled out a pouch of marbles, and tossed it into Ben's lap.

Ben grasped the pouch and raised his hand. "I'll come to visit."

Nathan stood and watched as the wagon bounced onto the main road and disappeared. Clenching his fists, he turned away. The shouts of the company men and a rising cloud of smoke drew him up Robinson Road. Of the big farms, now only Pa's, Duff's, and Murton's remained.

Mr. Hoople, the rail depot agent, had told him there were already over two hundred miners and their kin living in Manorville. "Italians, mostly," Mr. Hoople had said. "In fact, people are calling this town Little Italy. And more are coming from other mines. From Europe, too. Poles and Huns before long, I bet. In the whole region there're only about three hundred of us left, counting the babies. We're going to be outnumbered, for sure."

Nathan leaped into the weeds alongside the

road as two mule-drawn wagons piled high with lumber clattered past. The boys from Riggle's lumberyard drove one and Mr. Mueller from the general store the other. They didn't even wave. All anybody cared about now was making quick money, and there was plenty to be made building shanties. Even Mr. Hoople seemed glad. "At least, now the trains stop more than twice a week," he'd said.

Nathan tore off through the woods, heading toward the commotion in the Robinsons' fields. Near the edge of the woods, he spied a sycamore that had a blue shirt tied around it—Ben's school shirt. He saw the marks where Ben had dug up the leaf mold near the trunk—the secret place where he'd found all those arrowheads to trade.

Nathan squatted and sifted the dirt. He came up with an arrowhead right away. Good old Ben. Nathan gazed around at the thick-trunked trees as he slid the arrowhead deep into his pocket. The oldest farmers said that somewhere around here the Indians had made a last stand against the first British settlers—maybe on this very ridge.

Shouts, the snap of a whip, and the bray of mules made him step out from the trees.

In the hollow the company men had scalped the ground bare. The Robinsons' few cherry trees had been hacked down. As Nathan watched, the mules leaned into their harness to pull out the last

4

of the shrubbery. The Robinsons' white house and outbuildings rose high and ugly on the stripped earth. Some of the men hauled the last of the bushes to a huge smoldering heap from which the smoke rose. Other workers were pulling down the rotting fences and flinging the broken posts into the fire. One poured kerosene, and tongues of fire licked high.

Nathan felt the heat and choked on the smoke, but he didn't budge. Some crewmen ripped planks from the house and added them to the new lumber that Riggle's men and Mr. Mueller were unloading from the wagons. The company would knock those boards into shanties in no time.

The crew carried the doors and windows from the house to the lumber pile. Then the men attached ropes to the house and hitched them to a four-mule team. "Hey! Get up, you mules." The ropes went taut. The walls creaked and then splintered.

The ripping and the smashing tore at Nathan's gut. Suddenly, two sides of the house and the brick chimney collapsed with a roar, tearing open rooms. The high-pitched roof sagged.

The men began to scavenge lumber and bricks. Nathan grabbed a rock in each hand to hurl at the crew. He picked out a leather-skinned fellow with shaggy black hair—one of those foreigners. Nathan hefted the rock in his right hand. Pete Robinson would have just pitched the rock, clipped the fellow, and not cared.

A twig snapped and Nathan turned. Pa stood behind him. Nathan stuffed the rocks in his pockets.

Pa laid a hand on his shoulder. "Come away. I don't want you seeing this."

"I want to stay, Pa. I want to remember."

Pa turned him, but Nathan glanced back. The mules strained at the ropes again, planks went sailing, and the last walls toppled. The roof fell with a crash that shook the hollow. He should have thrown those rocks.

Pa drew him close. "Ma guessed where you were. You mustn't worry us. What's gotten into you?"

Nathan's stomach churned. "Why'd they have to build the shanties neighboring us?"

"Think about it, Nathan. The coal company's trying to make us sell. The company wants our land for the next shanty patch. Then the company will own everything on both sides of the main road for a mile—all the way to the Duff farm. They're even talking about putting another mine entry out here," Pa said, his voice rising as it had when his sister, Aunt Lydie, told him she was selling her acres. She'd been the first. Nearly a year ago, she took Uncle Herb and Cousin Verna away from

Manorville to live in Pittsburgh. And Ma's only surviving two sisters had gone days later. Now they sold handmade dresses to steel millionaires' wives and had become too highfalutin even to write to Ma.

Coal. King Coal. Nathan hated it. People called Manorville the boomtown of the 1890s. Coal was changing everything in western Pennsylvania—now even Manorville.

★ TWO ★

$\mathcal{P}$a hustled Nathan toward home. When they reached the white pickets surrounding their burying ground, Nathan tried to hurry past, but Pa went inside the fence and knelt by a small gravestone.

"Aw, Pa, not now," Nathan said under his breath. They'd been doing this for thirteen months. Sometimes, when Nathan came alone, he broke down and tears spilled—he did miss his brother. But he wouldn't bawl now in front of Pa. What good would that do? He swallowed hard to keep the tears from coming.

Nathan stared at the McClelland tombstones, at any but his brother's. He remembered Harry's big ears, freckles, and chipped-tooth grin. Harry had just started getting some height when he caught the fever. Pa believed he'd gotten sick after wading in the creek to spy on the engineering outfit that was surveying for the buildings at the new coal mine. Ma had told Harry to stay away from that camp and out of that dirty creek. He'd be fourteen now if only he'd listened to Ma.

"Maybe I should have sold out after Harry died," Pa murmured.

Sometimes Nathan felt he hardly knew his father anymore. He touched Pa's arm. "Come on, Pa. Let's get home. Ma'll be fretting." Ma would help him with his father. She never broke down, though Nathan knew she was still grieving, too.

"If I sell, the mine company promised to move the graves wherever we wanted—I've been thinking the churchyard near Ma's family might be all right."

"Maybe sell, then," Nathan mumbled, "if that'll end your hurting."

Pa nodded toward the tallest and oldest stone on the far end. "Would Great-Grandpa want that? This farm's all we know. But you with no brother or cousin or friends anymore—it's not fair to you, alone here with all these foreigners." He bowed his head.

Nathan bent so Pa had to look at him. Pa's eyes looked about to spill. His mouth was so down-turned his blond mustache drooped. Nathan cleared his throat and blurted out, "Come on, Pa. We've got to milk. The cows are needing us." Couldn't his father tell that he was growing up, that he could count on him, maybe even more than he had on Harry? Harry had always gotten into scrapes.

Nathan led the way to the lane. He could see their red brick house with the big barn, livery shed, and chicken coop nestled around it. The cows were heading to the barn through the broad meadows, ripe with early summer grasses. Their farm seemed sheltered, even safe. But above the distant trees toward Manorville, Nathan saw smoke rising from the steam engines at the mine.

When they entered the kitchen, they found Ma peeling potatoes for dinner. Her reddish hair stuck out of her kerchief. Her face glowed from gardening in the sun.

Her eyes, a blue brighter than Pa's, widened as she looked at Nathan. "Are you all right?"

"I was over at Ben Robinson's and . . ." Nathan began.

Ma suddenly walked around him to hug Pa. Pa's eyes were still tear-filled.

Nathan wanted to tell Ma what he'd seen at the Robinsons', but how could he now? He stood silent for a moment. Ma settled Pa into a chair and promised him that a cup of coffee would make him feel better. If only that would do it, Nathan thought. Finally, he said, "I'm going to put something in my room. Then I'll start the milking."

"You're a good boy, Nathan," Ma said, but she didn't turn from Pa.

Nathan took the back steps two at a time, hurried down the hall to his bedroom, and closed the door. He wanted to kick over his chair and pound the walls the way Ben and Pete would have—and Harry, too. He pulled the rocks from his pocket, wanting to throw them through the window. Maybe that would get Ma and Pa's attention. But he couldn't, not with them grieving so.

He drew a deep breath. He put the rocks down and worked the arrowhead from his pocket. He opened the walnut box that Pa had made for his and Harry's collection. He counted the arrowheads—now there were forty-seven. Most of them Harry and he had found together. He slammed the lid of the box.

With Harry's death, and now because of the coal company, there seemed no end to their troubles. If Harry were alive right now, he'd be bursting with schemes to help Ma and Pa.

Nathan groaned. Maybe he wasn't acting like a goody-goody only for his parents' sake. Maybe he was as lily-livered as Pete said he was and, to boot, a numskull who didn't know what to do.

★ THREE ★

*N*athan pressed his head into the cow's flank and milked faster. "Today's no different from any other," he muttered to himself. But every day was different—worse than the last. He had no one to pal around with. For the past few days, when he was allowed a second without chores, he'd spied on the coal company men knocking together shacks in Robinson Hollow. They were for Italian miners, Mr. Hoople told Pa. Then the miners had moved in. But today was the worst day of all. The miners were going to trespass on his family's property.

The shorthorn lowed. She turned to look at him. He milked more gently.

The steam whistle blasted, calling the miners. Nathan stopped milking and yelled out, "It's just not right!"

"Nathan, there's nothing we can do about it." Pa just kept milking.

"They should walk down Robinson Road."

"How many times do I have to tell you? The company showed me proof that we don't own the right-of-way. Our lane is just the shorter way to the mine."

"But it's McClelland Farm Lane. It's always been ours. Stop them, Pa!"

Pa didn't even look at him.

Nathan jumped up. Someone had to show some backbone. "I'll be right back." He sprinted out the door.

Nathan heard the miners' voices. Chimer leaped and bayed. The black-and-tan hound strained at his chain. Nathan ran through the front field, away from the house. He could see the miners in their raggedy denim jackets and pants, some with soft caps that had little lamps on the brim. Tin lunch pails swung from their arms. The miners were like a company of crows, covering his lane.

Nathan snatched up dried cow chips as he went and then darted toward the spruce trees along the fence. He'd make it so miserable for those miners, they'd be glad to walk the long way around on Robinson Road. Maybe tomorrow he'd turn Chimer loose on them.

He hurled the chips over the fence while trying to stay hidden in the trees. One chip landed right by the lead miner's feet. Another hit a man right in the chest. All the miners stopped, looking around and pointing. Two of them climbed the boards of the fence, burst through the brush, and ran at him. Nathan's heart pounded. He blindly hurled the last cow chip and ran. "Dirty foreigners!" he yelled.

The miners gained on him. They cut off his escape and edged him back toward the fence as if they were playing a game of tag.

The one closer to him had a handlebar mustache. Nathan dodged, but the man caught him, twisted a thick arm about his waist, and lifted him up.

Nathan's ribs ached. He punched the miner in the arm, but he didn't flinch. "Let me go," Nathan stammered. "Get off our land."

Ignoring his protests, the man hoisted Nathan over his broad shoulder. Hanging facedown over the miner's back, Nathan flailed, unable to get free. He tried to get a hand up to pull the man's hair but managed only to knock off his cap. "Put me down," Nathan choked. His stomach bounced on the man's shoulder, and the air went out of him. The long-legged miner clambered right over the fence with him.

"I'm not on your land now!" the fellow said, stomping about and showing Nathan to the other miners. They were all laughing. He was the butt of their joke, and he had done it to himself.

The farm bell clanged—Pa ringing him home. Nathan twisted and kicked, but the man only tightened his hold on him. "Please!" Nathan begged. Why could he never do anything right? Harry and Pete would have gotten away with it.

An older man with a long skinny face and graying hair came up beside them. He shouted in some foreign tongue—it must have been Italian—and tried to lift Nathan free and hand the fellow his cap and pail. Nathan reached out to the man, but the younger miner wouldn't let go. Nathan reared back, kicking and hitting, but the miner walked on, chuckling. Nathan's eyes began to water. He squeezed them shut. They weren't going to see him snivel.

The older man was shouting again. What was he saying? The man seemed to want to help him.

"*Si. Si.* I will put him down—my way," the miner said to the older man. He carried Nathan to the last fence post along the lane. The fellow hooked his fingers around the straps of Nathan's overalls and hung him from the post. The overalls pulled tight between Nathan's legs and against his stomach. He dangled forward, arms and legs thrashing.

The miner held a stubby finger under Nathan's nose. "The next time, you greet us nice." With other miners laughing around him, the man swaggered off down the lane, his head held high.

Nathan squirmed on the post as the rest of the miners filed past, grinning at him. He turned his head. He couldn't look them in the eye. In the distance the farm bell clanged. He wouldn't be in this fix if Pa had only stood with him. Ben's pap would have walloped any miner who grabbed Ben. He might have given Ben a few licks, too, for the trouble—but it would have been worth it.

The miner he'd hit in the chest with the cow chip stood before him. The man had dark circles under his eyes and his face showed hurt. Nathan found that he couldn't look away.

"I only come to this place for a job, and I do nothing to you," the man said. "You are a real bad boy, yes?"

Nathan shook his head, but before he could say anything, the man raised a cow chip. "You lose this, bad boy? I return to you." He crumpled it and stuffed it into Nathan's pocket. "Leave us alone," he said.

As he watched the fellow go, Nathan's cheeks burned. He was such a softy anybody could make him feel bad. Did any of those miners feel bad about trespassing and how they'd treated him? Nathan tried to reach the post with his hands and feet. If he could just boost himself up, he might get free. He almost got a hand on the top board, but he felt his overalls give. They were new. If they ripped, he'd have only hand-sewn flour sacks to wear until Ma took the time to mend them. He stayed still.

A boy with black hair that curled all the way down his neck ran back from the miners. His clothing bagged about his body. His face was so lean his eyes seemed to bug out.

"Leave me alone!" Nathan yelled, kicking his feet. "Get away!"

The boy looked scared but said, "Ernesto—he didn't mean you any harm. Let me help you. Quick, before he sees." The boy squatted and patted his shoulders.

Was this a trick to get everybody laughing again? Nathan wondered. He decided to take a chance. He set his feet on the boy to get a boost. The boy rose up, and Nathan lifted himself against the post, unhooked his straps, and jumped down. Once on the ground, Nathan took a long look at the boy. He seemed too young to be a miner, although he wore a miner's cap and lamp. Nathan guessed he was ten, but it was hard to tell—he was so short and scrawny. His jacket sleeves and pant legs had been rolled up to make them fit.

"You are fine?" the boy asked. He looked worried.

Nathan nodded.

The older man stood alone far down the lane. "Arturo," he called.

"Yes, Poppa." The boy ran to him.

Nathan wanted to pitch a rock at them, but he just watched them until they had disappeared onto the main road. Then he turned toward home, cleaning the dried manure out of his pocket. If he told Pa what'd happened, Pa would say he deserved it. Nathan's limbs felt weak and rubbery. There was no keeping the miners in their place. They were going to run all over his family's land, just the way they did everybody else's.

Anyway, he'd gotten a good look at one of the kids. Could a bundle of bones like that really work in the mine? And why had the kid bothered to come back to help him?

★ FOUR ★

The next dawn, Nathan stood at the barn door and peered at the miners heading down the lane to work. Pa didn't join him, but he didn't call him back inside, either. He was sitting on his milking stool, paging through the *Gallatin Gazette*, the county newspaper he'd picked up yesterday at the depot. He'd shown Nathan the photos of the bloodied passengers in a terrible Johnstown train wreck. The sorrow on Pa's face was almost worse than the photos. Nathan wanted to tell him, "We've had enough bad news without looking for more in the paper."

Suddenly, the boy, Arturo, sneaked from the line of miners and walked right into the front yard. Chimer bayed, pulling at the end of his chain, but the boy kept coming as if nothing frightened him.

Nathan inched from the barn door. The boy probably expected him to be grateful for helping him. Even if he was, he wasn't going to show it—not to some Italian.

Arturo grinned and waved him over as if they'd known each other all their lives. Before Nathan could decide what to do, Ernesto, the one who had hung him on the post, climbed over the fence. He yanked Arturo by the arm and smacked him a good one on the backside. Arturo tried to twist free, but Ernesto dragged him off.

"You rotten bully!" Nathan shouted. "Why don't you pick on somebody your own size?"

The man turned and his face reddened. Nathan took in how large the fellow really was, well over six feet tall with wide shoulders and big arms. He shook a thick index finger at Nathan. "You, is it? I watch for you. I teach you a good lesson next time."

Nathan slipped back into the barn. The last thing he needed was to become that bully's target every day. What did he care if that Ernesto beat the tar out of Arturo? But it wasn't a fair match. Arturo was so scrawny.

Nathan breathed in the warm scent of the barn—familiar and safe, as always. The shorthorns were waiting to be milked. But Pa slumped beside his cow, the newspaper thrown aside, his head bowed, and his hands motionless.

"Pa." Nathan laid a hand on his arm.

Pa shrugged off his hand without answering. He'd probably heard him outside and was peeved.

"One of those miners, a big one, was on our property, beating this kid who's just a runt. That's why I shouted and . . ."

His father glared at him. "Just stay away from them. I've told you what roughnecks they are."

Nathan kept his hands at his sides, wishing Pa would bear-hug him or tousle his hair the way he used to after he'd spoken sternly. But Pa didn't reach for him. Instead, he sighed and said, "Get to milking. We have more than enough to handle with our chores."

As Nathan started to milk, he said, "Pa, did you see the second hay is growing already? That's good news."

"And we'll have to hay alone again," Pa muttered. "I just don't know how we're going to keep up."

Spring haying without Uncle Herb and Aunt Lydie and the other farmers had taken days longer than usual. "I'll try to help even more," Nathan offered.

His father didn't say another word—not through the whole milking. Pa probably still thought he wasn't much help as a field hand.

As Pa carried the last of the pails of milk, he slipped and dropped one. He yelled and kicked the now empty pail against the barn wall.

Nathan kept his head down and kept on milking. He'd never seen his father act like that. He spoke up. "Pa, you always say, 'Next milking, there'll be another pailful where that one came from.' Are you all right?"

Pa snorted. "I'm doing dandy. Stick to business, or you'll spill a pail, for sure."

Nathan scowled. What had he done? He was always careful. He hadn't spilled a single drop in a year. Without another word, he helped his father set the milk to cool in the springhouse. Then, before Pa could order another chore before breakfast, Nathan bolted away from him into the sunlight.

Nathan stormed into the kitchen and burst out to Ma, "I do everything he wants, and he only acts grouchy with me."

The fine lines around Ma's eyes deepened. She fingered the biscuit dough as if she were seeking an answer in it. "I know your father's feeling down. And he keeps working so hard." She looked up from the dough. "It's Saturday. Maybe it'll cheer him up if we get away from the farm awhile. We'll go to the depot with him to deliver the milk. Then we can go up Main Street together and stop at Mr. Mueller's store."

Nathan hadn't gone to town with Pa since Ben

left. He wasn't so sure he wanted to go. "Do you think with the changes and all in town, Pa will really want to stay? All he does is unload the milk and head for home."

Ma rolled out the dough. "It's our going together again as a family. It'll remind him we can do more than work."

"Aw, Ma, I don't think Pa gives two hoots about much else—except, maybe, Harry."

Ma stared at him until Nathan murmured, "I'm sorry."

She studied her biscuit dough again. She picked up a water glass and repeatedly plunged it into the dough, making thick rounds. Nathan watched her punch her thumb into each round and fill the depression with jam from a jar that stood nearby. He had never seen her do that. "See," she said. "Something different. Maybe it'll work, maybe it won't . . . and maybe going together will brighten Pa's spirits. It can't hurt to try."

When Ma came out on the porch for the trip to town, she wore a fresh-laundered muslin dress, high button shoes, and a straw sunbonnet. It was the first time in over a year she hadn't worn black to town. Nathan thought she looked swell. She winked at him as he reached out to help her onto the wagon seat beside him. Maybe going would turn out to be a good idea. The filled biscuits had been a pretty good idea, even if he had burned his tongue on the bubbling jam.

Pa frowned, though, as she climbed up beside them. Ma just smiled and nudged Nathan. He turned to Pa and forced a grin. Pa stared ahead and then flicked Willie and Star's reins.

"It's a fine day, isn't it, David?" Ma said as they turned onto the lane.

Pa only offered, "Uh-huh."

Ma nudged Nathan again.

"You bet," he agreed. But Pa didn't look cheered by those words, either. He kept his eyes straight ahead and let Willie and Star amble down the tree-shaded lane.

"Why not show some stuff, Pa, like you used to?" Nathan finally said. "Make Willie and Star fly. It'll make everybody see who's coming."

His mother worked her elbow into him and shook her head. Nathan was so sick of being nudged and glared into silence. And Pa didn't pay attention, anyway. He let the horses amble. Pa was turning into an old grump. Nathan felt the sourness settling into himself, too. He didn't want to go any farther—seeing all the changes in town would only make him feel worse. But he sat trapped, his chest tightening, as the wagon swayed away from the farm.

FIVE

Willie and Star ambled around the last bend before town. On either side of the road the coal company had cut down all the trees. The clay was exposed, and ribbons of new railroad track gleamed over it. Beside the road women with bundles of clothes and food struggled along on foot. More buildings were going up in town. Men clambered over the scaffolds, hammering boards in place.

"My, it's busy, isn't it, Nathan?" Ma said, her voice weak.

Nathan stayed silent. It was awful. Coal dust stained the earth. In the distance, near the mine entrance, the new wooden coal tipple rose over the tracks. A steam locomotive was nudging rail cars, one after another in a long line, beneath the tipple. Nathan could see mules dragging loaded coal carts to the top of the tipple. When men tipped the carts, the coal showered down through the tipple into the waiting rail car. A cloud of black dust hovered over the whole area. The grass and trees on the nearby hills were yellowing. Nathan could tell from the set of Pa's jaw that he wasn't taking any of this well, either. How could he? How could any of them?

At the depot Nathan helped Pa unload the milk cans. Pa moved slowly and steadily, unlike Mr. Hoople, who was running along the platform with his freight lading sheets in hand. Nathan sped up, trying to step smart like Mr. Hoople, and pushed the milk cans into position for the train. Pa just dragged along.

Nathan eyed a woman in a rusty black dress, her head covered with a shawl. She had four kids with her, and battered cases and bundles were piled around her. A boy, about his own age, wearing a coat, knickers, and shoes, stared at him. The fellow had curly black hair like that boy Arturo.

"The trains are loaded with these immigrants," Mr. Hoople whispered. "This one says she's taking her brats away from here to Pittsburgh to live with her sister. Good riddance. But before you know it, there'll be ten more to replace them."

The boy looked Nathan up and down as if he was some kind of yokel who had never been anywhere. Well, he hadn't, but it wasn't his fault. Pa was turned, so Nathan made a fist.

Mr. Hoople stepped between the boy and him. "Are you crazy?" Mr. Hoople hissed and shoved him toward the wagon. "Big Jake Riggle from the lumberyard thought he could beat up one of them last night. Three of them jumped Big Jake and taught him a lesson. You'd better go along with your folks."

Nathan settled beside Ma on the wagon seat. Pa climbed aboard, took the reins, and called "Hey," to Willie and Star. Nathan looked hard at the boy on the platform as they rolled toward Main Street.

"Nathan! What's gotten into you, staring at somebody like that?" Ma asked, elbowing him.

"You'd better mind your Ma," Pa said.

Why couldn't they understand how he felt? When they used to come to town, the few people around smiled and greeted them by name. Now, everywhere he looked, new people swarmed on the dirt street and on the wooden sidewalks. They ignored him and his family—treated them as if *they* were the strangers.

When they got to Mr. Mueller's store, it was crowded with immigrants. Stony-faced men and women stood in line before the counter. Some of the women had crying babies on their hips. The smell of sweat and spices mingled in the store.

Mr. Mueller moved fast, measuring flour and sugar into sacks. He had a new clerk, who moved even faster, cutting ribbons and yard goods and making change. The aisles and floor were stacked with new merchandise. Mr. Mueller was the only one smiling.

Ma and Pa shrank to the side, acting as timid as rabbits, but Nathan wasn't going to let his family be ignored here. He waved at Mr. Mueller. Finally, he came over to them and took the small crate of eggs Ma had brought to barter. His broad red face beamed. "Thank you. I can sell all you bring. I'm busier every day." Pa was, too, Nathan thought, but he wasn't happy about it.

"I'm sorry you had to wait," Mr. Mueller went on.

"Oh, they were here before us," Ma said quietly.

"Most of them don't spend enough to matter. The company's setting up a store for them. But the mine engineers and the managers spend." He pulled out some new bolts of cloth.

Ma fingered the yard goods. She'd love a dress length, Nathan could tell, but she said, "Not today."

Nathan lowered his head. They were always saving against something bad at the farm. If they didn't buy, Mr. Mueller would think they were nobodies, like the immigrants.

"No time as good as today," Mr. Mueller said, smiling. "Your credit's good with me, if that's a problem. All David has to do is sell the farm and get into some other line of trade. You'll have money to buy anything you want."

"We don't buy on credit," Pa said softly.

"It's the 1890s," Mr. Mueller said. "Don't be so old-fashioned. You ought to see the plans for the houses the managers are building up on the ridge. I'm thinking of moving my family there. No more living above the store for us. You have to change with the times."

Nathan saw his father shake his head. Pa change? Never! Nathan stalked out of earshot. He watched the clerk fill a candy sack for a little immigrant boy. There wouldn't be a sack like that for him.

Nathan had seen enough. He wanted fresh air, so he slipped out the door onto the back porch. The coal company had expanded the mine yard closer to the rear of the store. Since Harry had died, Nathan had seen each frame building completed—mule barn, tool and wash-up shed, office, tipple, and above the mine entrance the tiny building that housed the steam-driven fan that blew air into the mine. The yard around the mine entrance had been rimmed with a flimsy post-and-wire-mesh fence. When it was put up, townspeople had half-joked that they wanted something stronger to hold the miners in.

Some company workers led mules that were pulling the coal-filled carts away from the mine entry. Near the tipple he saw a couple of boys sorting shale from coal piles. They were too tall to be that Arturo. Nathan wondered how they stood the racket from the clattering ventilator fan, the coal rattling down into the empty cars, the clunk of the railroad cars bumping ahead, the shrill whistle of the little steam engine that tugged the wooden cars.

On the porch near Nathan two fellows, lounging against a post, glared at the miners. Nathan thought he recognized one of them as the owner of a farm near White Valley. His throat ached—at least somebody familiar. But they ignored him—probably thought he didn't count for much.

"Those dogs ganging up on a man like Riggle," the man who looked familiar growled to the other. "It's time we taught 'em their place. Some of the boys have a mind to get together and corner a few. Can we count on you?"

"You bet you can. If we bash some heads and break some bones, they'll learn who's boss."

Breaking bones? Nathan stepped back.

The man Nathan had not seen before suddenly turned and stared at him.

Nathan eased toward the door.

"Who's this eavesdropping—one of them?" the stranger hissed. "Grab him before he tells."

The other man stopped his friend but took hold of Nathan's shoulder. "Now, just look at this boy, ya fool. He's not going to go blabbing what he heard, are you? You're one of us, ain't ya, boy?"

Nathan wanted to shout, "No, I'm not!" But he stayed quiet and nodded.

"And ya don't have any pals among them that ya'd squeal to, do ya?"

Nathan shook his head slowly.

The man looked at him a long moment and then released his shoulder. Nathan opened the door and backed into the store. He got beside Ma and Pa. He stared at the immigrants with their weary, lined faces. They pushed and demanded. Mr. Mueller and his clerk swaggered and smiled and rang the cash register again and again.

The two toughs entered the store and eyed everyone. Nathan was glad he wasn't like them. But he'd *acted* like them. He had glared at that boy at the depot and would have knocked him down if he could have. And didn't he want to chase the miners from his lane—even set Chimer on them? The men passed, shoving him against some immigrant women. The women grumbled at Nathan. He felt trapped among them all. As soon as Mr. Mueller handed Ma her measly packets of flour and sugar in exchange for the eggs, Nathan pushed his way outside to the wagon with his parents following.

As they rolled toward home, he didn't speak and neither did Ma or Pa. Nathan looked at all the immigrants and townsfolk jostling in the road—poisoned-looking and spiteful. He didn't want to be like any of them. He didn't want to join anybody's gang and sneak around at night to beat up people. He didn't want to act sour and spiteful, either. He glanced behind once or twice. Was that pair trailing to find out who he was and if he'd squeal to cause trouble? He didn't catch sight of them.

When they got home, Nathan helped Pa unharness and cool Willie and Star. Then, without waiting for his parents to ask him, he grabbed a hoe and went out to the vegetable bed to till. Aside from the birds trilling and the hens clucking, the garden was peaceful after all that racket in town. He worked the hoe fast along the rows of sprouting beans, beets, squash, and carrots—back and forth, back and forth, like the piston of a steam engine. He could feel his muscles burn. He was getting stronger. They could grow lots of vegetables, and they could buy more laying hens. They could sell the eggs and vegetables to Mr. Mueller. They could stay out here on the farm alone, away from everyone.

The spruce branches near him parted, and Arturo stepped out. He was covered with grime, but his black eyes gleamed. He stuck out his hand. "Shake hands?"

Nathan wanted to shout and tell him to go. Arturo smiled. Nathan couldn't manage a sound, and he pushed the hoe blade into the ground.

Chimer bayed. Ernesto was climbing into the yard below. Nathan felt his heart beat faster.

Arturo stood with his hand still outstretched. He was going to get another pounding just for being friendly.

Nathan pointed to Ernesto. He was looking toward the lower yard and fields. He hadn't seen them.

"My brother!" Arturo breathed.

That bully—Arturo's brother? Nathan stared at Ernesto, but he was still looking the other way, toward the cows.

Nathan pulled Arturo into the trees. Hidden by the pricking spruce branches, Nathan crouched with him.

"Tomorrow is Sunday," Arturo whispered. "I don't work. Meet me in the woods by my house. I will sneak away."

Nathan pressed his finger to his lips and shook his head from side to side. Didn't Arturo realize he might be heard? That bully might smack them both.

"You know where the big trees are?" Arturo whispered. "You come."

Nathan hit his finger against his lips. Beyond

the fence, he could hear the miners talking as they headed toward the hollow. "Good. You will come," Arturo murmured and then slid out of the branches toward the lane.

Nathan froze. Ernesto was going to fall on Arturo. But no sound of shouts or blows came.

Nathan stuck his head out. The yard and lane were empty, so he went back to his hoeing. Poor Arturo—having Ernesto for a brother. Nathan knew what it was like to be bossed and pounded by an older brother. But Ernesto was a lot worse than Harry—or even Pete. He was more like that pair at Mr. Mueller's store.

Nathan stopped hoeing and stood up straight. Arturo had surprised him, so he'd never thought of warning him about those men planning to bash miners. Shouldn't he run after Arturo? But then he decided against it. He wasn't like those men at the store. But he wasn't about to get friendly with some Italian kid, either.

★ SIX ★

*N*athan moved his scrambled eggs around the plate with his fork. He felt as if he hadn't slept a wink. All night he'd been waking up, worrying. Maybe he should meet with Arturo today to warn him.

"Nathan, quit dawdling. You're going to make us late for the morning service," Ma said, stacking her and Pa's plates.

"I don't think it matters to the Lord if I miss the service today," Pa said, staring at the table.

Nathan's stomach tightened. Nobody missed church unless he was sick. That was his mother's rule.

Ma walked back to the table. She was already in a Sunday dress, a dark one, but not black. She looked bothered, but her voice sounded soothing. "Now, David, the service will make you feel better."

Pa glanced out the window. "Annie, it'll make me feel worse to sit in a near-empty church and be reminded that three-quarters of the congregation has moved away. I need to rest awhile. I'll read my *Gazette*. Then the cultivator needs to be put through the cornfields."

"Lately, all you dwell on is the bad news in that paper," said Ma. "You'd be better off reading your Bible. And there's no work that needs doing on the Sabbath." She sounded just like Nathan's Sunday school teacher. When Pa didn't look at her, she said, "Well, Nathan and I are going. Nathan, get up those stairs and get dressed, and then bring the buggy."

Nathan wanted to stay with Pa, but that would send Ma on the warpath, for sure. He took the steps two at a time, not wanting to hear if they had words. He hadn't eaten much, but his stomach hurt. And he still didn't know what to do about warning Arturo. He wouldn't think about it now. He fastened his collar and string tie just right. He pulled his socks up to his knickers and laced his shoes.

Nathan's stomach was still in knots as he hitched Willie. Ma was standing on the kitchen steps when he pulled up in the buggy. He reached out his hand to help her onto the seat. She wore a straw bonnet with flowers, one he hadn't seen since before Harry's funeral. "That looks nice," Nathan murmured as she settled beside him.

She nodded. Pa didn't come outside. Ma motioned for Nathan to go, and he guided Willie away from the porch. Ma stared straight ahead, her shoulders squared, her lips set. She could be just as silent as Pa.

As they reached the main road, his eyes began to tear up so that he could barely see. Willie ambled on as if he knew where he was taking them. "Ma," Nathan burst out, "when does a person stop grieving?"

For a long time she didn't answer. She sat stiffly, looking away. "I don't think there's a short or long to it, Nathan," she said finally. "For the rest of our lives, we'll all miss Harry. You will, too." She sighed and looked right at him. "I guess the hard grieving stops when you can really look at the ones who are still with you and hope that life's not all about los-ing." She put her hand on his shoulder. "Then you start living more for them, instead of just missing the one you've lost."

He did miss Harry—sometimes so much he could hardly stand it. He leaned into Ma. "But what about Pa? Will he get to feeling that way, too?"

She looked toward the town. "He's grieving Harry, for sure, but he's also trying to sort out all these other changes, too. He's having his first real losses. I suppose we just have to keep reminding him how much we need him. Don't be too hard on him, promise?"

Nathan nodded. Ma wiped her eyes with a hankie. "That's enough, now, Nathan, you hear? You'll have me blubbering, and I just won't."

He kept still. By the time they drew up to the church and he helped her from the buggy, any sign of her tears was gone. She picked up her skirts and marched forward. Nathan noticed she didn't allow herself her usual moment of silence beside the churchyard where most of her kin were buried. He marched right on beside her. At the church steps Mrs. McMurty, the minister's wife, smiled into Nathan's face, shook his hand, and then asked where his father was. Nathan felt his face going red and turned away.

Ma raised her chin and said, "David's feeling poorly. Thank you for asking."

Nathan entered a nearly empty Sunday school. He was hoping to see any familiar boy, even one from as far away as White Valley. Rhetta and Rheena Mueller came in. He waved. Instead of coming to sit with him, they snubbed him and sat in the front row. Some other girls arrived, but no boys. He wondered if more farmers had sold out and there really were no more fellows his age left to pal around with.

To begin the lesson Mrs. Lemmon, their white-haired teacher, asked what birds around Manorville migrated every fall. The girls called out, "Robins. Geese. Orioles. Finches. Ducks." Then Mrs. Lemmon asked if each spring any ever failed to return to Manorville.

The girls giggled, and guessed some that might not. Nathan knew they were joshing with Mrs. Lemmon, so he raised his hand. "They all return every spring." Then he recited the Scripture passage about the birds of the air and not one falling without the Creator caring. Ma always kept at him about memorizing more passages.

Rheena turned and stuck out her tongue, but he ignored her. Mrs. Lemmon had folded some paper into the shape of birds, and now she handed them out. That was for little kids, so he didn't bother to listen anymore. At least he'd shown up and knew the Bible verses.

He was pleased Ma decided to leave before the shared lunch and the afternoon service. But as he drove the buggy home through the empty Sunday fields, he felt awfully alone—like a sparrow that had migrated home to find only crows.

When he and Ma reached the farm, he didn't see Pa in the near fields or in the livery shed. After settling Willie in his stall, Nathan changed out of his Sunday clothes. Ma met him in the kitchen with a worried look. "I'm not seeing your father. Find him, will you, while I start preparing dinner?"

Pa wasn't in the vegetable patch or the barn. Nathan shaded his eyes and scanned the far meadows—not there, either. Pa was at their burying ground again, Nathan decided. Just great. And he was going to have to fetch him.

As Nathan headed to tell Ma, she gestured to him from the kitchen porch. "I found him. He's resting in the parlor." She sounded unsettled. No wonder, Nathan thought. Pa wasn't much for afternoon resting.

"Why don't you see if he'll get up for you?" Ma said. "I already tried."

Pa was lying still on the settee, the newspaper scattered on the floor. In the light seeping around the window shades, Nathan could see that his father's eyes were open. Nathan almost jumped on him to wrestle the way they used to, but when he moved close, Pa didn't glance up. "Pa," Nathan asked, "how about going fishing?"

"Not today, Nathan."

"How about taking Chimer for a run in the woods and doing some shooting? We haven't done that in an age."

Pa shook his head. "I'm tuckered out, Nathan. Today's a day for rest—Ma was right."

But Nathan really wanted to tell him about the

men at Mueller's and ask whether he should warn the immigrants. "Pa, something happened in town that I wanted to talk to you about."

Pa raised his hand. "Not now, Nathan." He closed his eyes.

That stung. Pa wouldn't even *listen* to him. Nathan stomped out of the parlor into the kitchen. Ma raised an eyebrow, but he went outside without saying anything and sat on the kitchen steps. He wanted to shout to break the quiet. He stared over the meadow toward the woods on the ridge and Robinson Hollow.

Ma stepped onto the porch and put her hand on Nathan's shoulder.

At least she always stuck by him.

"I'm sorry. I suppose that everybody has to sort it all out in his own way. We just have to give Pa more time."

More time—how could they be sure there'd be more? Harry had run out of time. Even the country-side seemed to be running out of time. But none of them did anything. At least he could tell Ma about the men at Mueller's store and ask her what he should do.

"Annie," Nathan heard Pa call from inside the house.

Ma turned and started in.

Nathan stood and looked toward the trees on

the ridge. Since they wouldn't listen, maybe he needed to make some decisions on his own. He started down the steps. "Go in, Ma. I need to go off and explore awhile, anyway."

"Nathan," Ma's voice quavered. "You're not going to get into any devilment?"

"Naw." He headed toward the meadow, not bothering to turn when she called him again. Arturo was probably gone by now. But if he was there, Nathan would warn him. It would be real easy for the men to plan an ambush from the woods along the lane. Maybe he'd tell Arturo that the long way around on Robinson Road would be safer to travel because the trees had been torn out. If the miners believed all that, then he'd have warned them *and* they'd be off his lane, too.

★ SEVEN ★

After Nathan crested the hill and started into the woods, he slowed. Maybe it was all a trick, and it would be Ernesto who was waiting for him. He crept through the copse, trying not to stir a leaf.

Near Ben's sycamore he saw someone. Arturo. He was sitting alone beside a fallen tree, thumping it with a stick as he stared at the sky.

Nathan watched him. He looked scrawnier than ever. He wore the same faded denims he did for work, but now with a torn blue shirt. His feet were bare. Nathan thought of just sneaking back to the farm. But what was the good of that—he'd just sit alone all day. And Arturo *had* waited for him.

Nathan eased from his hiding place. "I couldn't get here any sooner."

Arturo showed most of his teeth in a smile. "But you came. Sit. Tell me, please, your name."

Nathan sank down, stuck out his hand, and told him.

He pumped Nathan's hand. "I am Arturo Tozzi."

"I can't stay. I only came to warn you. I overheard some men in town saying a gang was going to waylay some miners—on my farm lane," he added. "Did anybody get beat up last night?"

Arturo shook his head. His eyes had widened, but he shrugged. "It happens everywhere," he muttered, looking sad.

"Well, I've got to go. Just be sure and tell everybody. The men could jump out from the trees on the lane. Robinson Road might be safer."

"Wait. Don't go." Arturo reached into his back pants pocket and pulled out a slingshot. He laid it in Nathan's hand. "A present. My poppa made it from a rubber belt that broke at the mine."

Nathan stared, surprised. He tried to hand the slingshot back. "But I can't take your—"

Arturo wouldn't accept it. "Yes. Yours now. Try it. Such strong rubber." He put pebbles in Nathan's hand. "It hits a target. Try."

Nathan selected a pebble and then drew back on the stiff sling, took careful aim, and let go. The pebble soared through the leaves and hit the cleft of Ben's sycamore. He shot again and hit it. "Wow! But I can't keep . . ."

"Yes, for you." Arturo closed Nathan's fingers about the slingshot.

Nathan fiddled with it, then slid it into his pocket. "Thanks," he said at last.

Arturo sifted dirt through his fingers. "Some men in town say our houses are near an old Indian village. One even showed me an arrowhead he said he found out here. I think he was trying to scare me. I know the Indians are gone, but I liked that arrowhead. Do you think we could find some?"

Nathan guessed that Arturo would get plenty excited if he learned there was a treasure trove of arrowheads all around them. He decided he'd keep that his and Ben's secret. Instead, he asked, "Do you really work in the mine?"

"Do you know the town Connellsville? I work in the mine there since I was seven. I pick the slate out of the coal for Poppa and my brother, Ernesto. At the mine here," he said, sounding proud, "most of the time I am the trapper boy."

"What animals can you trap in the mine?"

"No, no. Traps are like doors. I open and shut them to get the good air where the men work. The mine air can get bad if I do not open and shut the traps."

"Is it hard work?" Nathan asked.

"It's easy work, but I sit alone most days. But I

talk too much about me. Your poppa owns the farm? You work with him?"

Nathan lifted his head, determined not to be outdone. "Sure, I milk the cows, feed the horses and chickens. We have a pig. I work in the fields." He watched Arturo—he seemed impressed.

"You have so many beautiful animals to be with. And your big house. You must be very rich."

"No. My family bought the land a long time ago. Back then, land here cost pennies."

"No, you are rich. My poppa told me he worked on a farm in Tuscany in Italy. He worked with animals, but he could never own. Only the rich own the land, the animals. Poppa brought us to this country for Ernesto and for me. Poppa says even as a boy Ernesto wants to own animals. I was very young, so I do not remember."

Nathan shrugged, but he felt pleased. Pa acted like they were becoming nobodies, but Arturo thought they were big shots.

"Do you have lots of friends around the town?" Arturo asked.

Nathan shook his head. "Most days I spend alone, too," he admitted. "My friends have moved away. Do you have lots of pals in the hollow?"

"No. Many of the men still wait to bring their families here. Soon they will come. There are some babies. Most miners here are older than me. They don't want to be with me, and me, maybe I don't want to be with them—always doing the same things, sticking together in the company patch, not speaking English. Me, I want to learn. I try to make friends—like with you. You want to see the hollow? Come on. I'll show you."

Arturo grabbed Nathan's arm, pulled him to his feet, and dragged him through the woods toward the shanties. Nathan dug in his heels. "Whoa! Not so fast. Maybe we shouldn't. What about your brother? What if he sees me with you?"

"Come on, *per favore*. Ernesto, my brother, he's not there. He will not catch us. Come, please." Arturo's black eyes challenged him. "You're not scared?"

Nathan stuck out his chest. No pint-sized foreigner was going to say that to him. And he had wanted to do something different. Pa wouldn't like it, but he hadn't offered anything else. "Let's go."

He followed Arturo down the ridge and through the yellow dust to the shanties. Somewhere a fiddle squealed a tune. Men laughed and talked as they rolled wooden balls in the dust. "*Bocce*—a game," Arturo said. "They play for hours."

As Nathan passed, the men stared. Did they recognize him? One pointed, and the others talked and laughed. Nathan couldn't understand a word. One man stepped forward. He looked like the one who had stuffed the cow chip in Nathan's overall pocket.

"Don't worry. As long as you are with me, no one will bother you," Arturo said. The man's friends pulled him back to the game.

Nathan stayed in step with Arturo. The company houses were uglier up close—all ill-fitting boards, small windows, sagging doors, steep roofs with tin stovepipes sticking through. The narrow houses were perched on wooden posts. Underneath some of the shacks, water oozed—it smelled of human waste. Maybe their outhouse pits hadn't been dug deep enough.

Arturo led him toward a house at the row end. "This is the best place," he declared. The house was bright blue and looked newly painted, and sweet peas on strings had started to grow up to the porch rail. On the porch a man leaned back in a chair, his sock-covered feet resting on the rail. He had shaggy black-and-gray hair and a long thin nose. He smoked a corncob pipe, like the one of Grandpa's that Pa kept on his bureau. The man looked familiar. Yes, it was the older fellow who had tried to lift him free that day Ernesto had grabbed him like a sack of potatoes. Nathan hung back, but Arturo nodded at him.

Nathan set his jaw and marched up the three steps to the porch.

Arturo gestured to the man. "My poppa, *Signor* Alberto Tozzi." He talked in Italian to his father, and Nathan made out his own name.

Mr. Tozzi looked surprised, but he leaned forward and gripped Nathan's hand in both of his. His hands were calloused and scrubbed red. When Mr. Tozzi grinned, he looked just like Arturo.

The door banged open, and a woman and a girl walked out, both wearing black scarves over their hair. "*Mia madre,*" Arturo said. "My mother and my sister, Teresa."

Arturo's family spoke in Italian, and Nathan shifted from one foot to the other.

Arturo turned from them to him. "Momma asks will you stay to eat with us, please? The food is soon ready."

Did he want to go that far—to eat their food or even see the inside of their shanty? He could smell garlic, onions, tomatoes—the hollow's new odors. He'd just end up sitting like a blockhead while they jabbered at each other in Italian. "No. Thank you, no." Nathan went down the steps. "Tell your family my mother cooked supper. She'll worry if I don't get home."

Nathan could tell Arturo felt let down, but the rest of them looked happy to be let off the hook.

They smiled and waved. He was doing them a favor—they probably didn't have enough food.

Arturo leaped from the steps. "I will walk with you part way." He still looked bothered. "My poppa," he mumbled after a second, "he asks if you will still throw things at us when we walk the lane."

Nathan felt his face redden. "No," he stammered.

"I already told him so. You will come again?"

He hadn't intended to come at all, let alone again. But he'd never been around anyone so eager to be his friend, not even Ben. They were passing the *bocce* game. The same man glanced at Nathan and shook his fist.

Nathan began to trot, but Arturo kept pace beside him. "You will come, won't you?" His mouth had turned down.

Nathan saw the meadows and his own house. Arturo looked so dejected, Nathan blurted out, "How about this—do you want to meet me at the farm sometime to see the cows and horses?"

"Yes!" Arturo leaped around him, grinning again. "Maybe tomorrow night, if I am not late from the mine and Poppa says it's all right." He ran off, waving.

"Meet me in the trees by the fence," Nathan called after him. After Arturo vanished, Nathan still stared into the hollow. He'd bet Arturo wanted the invitation all along. And he'd also bet Pa and Ma would have plenty to say if they saw Arturo. Nathan shrugged—he wasn't so sure he really cared. At least, he'd spent his afternoon doing more than working, staring at cows, and acting sulky like Pa.

★ EIGHT ★

The next evening Arturo hustled into the trees beside Nathan. He was breathing hard. "I run all the way. Am I safe here?"

"Sure. Why not?" Nathan asked.

"Last night, men chased Ernesto's friends."

Nathan's breath caught. The two men from Mueller's store—they or somebody like them were at it. "What happened?"

"They walked home late at night on Robinson Road. I warned them about the lane, like you said. They run fast and get away. They say from now on they stick to the lane—it's safer. They take cover behind the trees."

Nathan shook his head. It figured—no scheme of his ever worked.

"Poppa said I should not visit," Arturo said, "but no one will hurt somebody like me, right? I just wanted so much to see the animals."

Nathan knew he could get rid of Arturo with a warning, but the kid acted so keen on seeing the animals, he couldn't disappoint him. Besides, Nathan had already figured out that Ma and Pa wouldn't catch sight of Arturo if he led him inside the livery shed. "Stay. Nobody will hurt you as long as you're with me. Do you want to see the horses?"

When Arturo peered at Willie and Star through the stall doors, he didn't look worried anymore. "Nathan, bring one out."

Nathan put a halter on Willie and led the bay into the shed aisle. Arturo walked right up to the big horse. He only stood half the height of Willie's chest, but he reached and rubbed Willie's nose. Willie shook his head and blew on Arturo's hand. "He's so fine," Arturo said. "Let me brush him."

"That's doing chores."

"Not for me. Please, let me."

Nathan laughed—it'd been a long time since he had seen anybody on the farm with a grin so wide. He put Willie in the crossties, handed Arturo a brush, and watched him clamber on the stool to work. "I thought you said you were never around horses."

"I said my poppa never owned one. I go around barns to see the animals. There's the mule barn at the mine. Poppa won't let me work with the mules because he's afraid I get kicked." He brushed until

Willie's bay coat gleamed, and his mane and tail were full. He grinned at Nathan. "Can I ride him now?"

Arturo had done such a great grooming job, Nathan figured he owed it to him. He peeked out the door. Sunset was coming. If he led Willie fast to the upper meadow, Ma and Pa probably wouldn't see. Nathan clipped a rope to the halter. "Climb on," he told Arturo.

Nathan led Willie behind the shed and into the field with Arturo on bareback, clinging to the mane. Still grinning, Arturo reached down. "Let's ride him together."

Nathan was just about to climb up when he saw a man running toward them from the shadows beneath the trees. Was it one of the townsmen? Nathan wanted to run, but held his ground, lean-ing into the big horse. It was Ernesto, and he was on them in no time. He hauled Arturo off the horse and began shouting at him in Italian.

Arturo struggled in his arms. He called to Nathan, "Poppa's worried someone will hurt me. I'll come another night for a ride."

Nathan stepped forward to say that no one would hurt him, but Ernesto leaned down, his eyes wide and his mouth twisted beneath his mustache. He roared right in Nathan's face, "No! He will *not* come again. You stay away from each other!"

Ernesto straightened and smacked Willie on the rump.

Willie leaped, dragging Nathan. Nathan grasped the lead rope, tugging with all his strength. Willie stopped but pranced in place. As Nathan quieted the horse, Ernesto disappeared with Arturo through the trees.

Leading Willie back to the shed, Nathan stared at the shadows. He'd never felt edgy on the farm, but Ernesto had fallen on them in a moment. Anybody could have—even the pair from the store. It wasn't fair to Arturo—or to him. They were having a good time.

In the distance a train whistled, a cold, lonesome sound. He listened to scurrying and cracking in the brush. The shadows were lengthening, swallowing the field, and he hurried Willie into the shed.

Three days later, after sticking to the farm and his chores, Nathan sat alone on the kitchen steps. The branches of the nearby spruce stirred. Chimer growled. Nathan grabbed Ma's broom and held it ready as he backed toward the house. Suddenly, Arturo's face poked out. He beckoned at Nathan, who breathed easy and grinned. Chimer barked, but Nathan shushed him. He crawled to Arturo in the trees. "How did you get away?" Nathan whispered.

"Ernesto thinks I gather wood for Momma near the hollow."

"Are you sure nobody saw you?"

Arturo shook his head. "I stayed in the shadows and ran. I came for a minute to say hello." He raised his chin and his eyes gleamed.

He'd gotten one over on Ernesto and was proud of it, Nathan realized. Arturo had some spunk.

"Why didn't you visit me?" Arturo asked.

"Your brother—why's he chasing after us and all?"

Arturo hung his head. "Ernesto, he worries. He wants me to stay with my own people, so I don't get beat up. He hates it that I'm always trying to meet people outside of the company houses and that I learn to speak English pretty good—better than him, anyhow. Don't worry about Ernesto. Momma always says her milk must have been very good when he was a baby. He's like a bull. He rages, always angry. 'This is bad and that will be bad,' he roars. But Momma and Poppa keep him fenced. Poppa says that when Ernesto can afford to bring his bride from Italy, he will be nicer. You come visit the hollow, all right?"

Not with Ernesto snorting and pawing around, Nathan decided. He knew a lot about bulls, and nobody could ever tame them. "I have chores. . . . How about this? You meet me Sunday about four o'clock in the lower meadow. I'll hide in the bushes by the pond."

"If I tell Poppa it's just for the afternoon and I'll be safe, he'll maybe let me. Poppa understands me. I have to go back now."

They crawled to the edge of the lane. No one was lurking there. Arturo took off as Nathan watched. Arturo's black denims marked him as one of them—and the dark hair that straggled down his neck. If only Arturo looked different. That was it! He could get Arturo to look more like a regular fellow. Nobody would bother him then. Ma and Pa might not even care if Arturo became a pal.

On Sunday when Arturo crawled into the bushes near the pond, Nathan was ready. "I have a game I want to teach you." He opened his penknife. "Mumblety-peg. I'll bet it was a game Indian boys played."

"Indians?" With that big grin of his, Arturo studied the knife. Nathan showed him how to set the blade point on his fingers, palm, elbow, and shoulder, and each time fling the knife so the blade would stick in the ground. "If you miss, you have to pull a matchstick out of the mud with your teeth." He pushed the matchstick in only halfway—he and Ben always had to eat dirt because Pete and Harry buried it to the tip.

After only two tries, Arturo flung the knife and the blade stuck in the ground. After twenty minutes Arturo only once had to put his face to the ground to pull out the matchstick—and he laughed. Ben would have pitched a fit. Arturo started to practice making the knife do a flip before it stuck in the ground.

"Let's go swimming," Nathan said. He skinned out of his overalls to his underdrawers.

Arturo backed from the edge of the pond. His eyes were wide with worry. "I cannot swim. I will just play with the knife."

Nathan grabbed his arm. "Come on. I'll teach you. All the boys around here swim." He tried to shove Arturo into the pond.

"Nathan, I cannot get wet the clothes I wear in the mine. I have to go home now."

"Wait! Don't go. It won't matter if you get your pants wet. You can take them off to dry. Here, I brought you a present." From under a bush Nathan pulled an old flour sack. "Look inside."

Arturo sat away from the water. He opened the sack. "Overalls like yours!" he cried.

Nathan was sure that his outgrown pair would fit Arturo. "They're my old ones, but they don't have any holes," he said. "And if you'll let me have my knife back, I'll use it to cut your hair short like mine."

Arturo stared at him and then nodded slowly.

"Well, let's go swimming first." A good soaking might lighten Arturo's skin.

Arturo was moving toward the pond when Nathan heard talking. Ma and Pa strolled around the bushes. Nathan froze.

He saw his father's jaw set and his face get red. Pa hissed something in Ma's ear and tried to guide her away.

Nathan brought Arturo nearer. "Ma and Pa, this is Arthur."

"My name is Arturo."

Arturo definitely had a lot to learn. Pa just frowned.

Arturo whispered in Nathan's ear, "Your pa does not want me here?"

Ma stepped forward and stuck out her hand. "Pleased to meet you, Arturo. Nathan, pull on your overalls and you two come to the house for cake."

At least Ma could be counted on. Arturo gave her that wide smile. Nathan knew if Arturo kept that up, he'd sure melt Ma.

Nathan saw Pa raise an eyebrow as if questioning what Nathan was doing. Then he stomped away, muttering, "I have to check a fence."

All this time Nathan had thought Pa was just worn down from all the changes—but now he wondered if Pa was turning just as spiteful as those men at Mr. Mueller's store. Arturo couldn't do any real harm, and after Nathan gave him a few more lessons, why he'd almost pass for a country boy. Pa couldn't be much bothered by him then.

★ NINE ★

Pa spoke little the next morning, and he took
the milk to the depot alone. When he came inside
to eat lunch, he finally said, "I don't understand
what you're up to, Nathan. You're the one who
acted like you couldn't abide the miners. Now
you're bringing them around. I'd rather that miner
boy not feel he can traipse all over my property."

"Shame on you, David!" his mother said, her
eyes wide. "He's only a boy—a boy who's nice.
How could you close your door to him?"

Pa's head went up. "I don't want any problems.
Mr. Hoople said there was a knife fight the other
day. This boy's only going to bring more trouble to
the farm. And he's not a fit friend for our only son,
Annie. The miners are not like us, any of them."

Nathan felt a twinge in his stomach. "I'm
teaching him, Pa. He can learn to be like me.
You'll see. He'll be no problem."

Ma stroked Pa's hand. "Maybe it isn't good Nathan spends so much time alone."

"He has friends. Mr. Hoople told me that Ben and Pete came on the train last week to help their Uncle Shep and Aunt Myrt." Then he turned to Nathan and said, "Your friends are visiting in White Valley. If you'll be patient, we'll get over to see them."

Nathan leaped up.

"But they'll have to go back," Ma said, stacking the plates.

Nathan didn't care. He just wanted to be with real friends. "When can we go? This afternoon? Please, Pa, it's only five miles."

His father didn't look at him. "Well, I've got to finish cultivating the corn. It's knee-high with these warmer nights. And you have peas to pick and shuck with Ma, and there's the vegetable bed to hoe. Just as soon as I feel caught up, we'll drive Willie over."

"Maybe this evening, Pa? Or tomorrow?"

Pa nodded. "Maybe we'll all go fishing, too."

Nathan headed for the door. "Let's get working." He wouldn't stop until the chores were done—not even to see Arturo.

That night and then the next, Pa didn't come out of the cornfields until dusk and Nathan still had hoeing in the garden. At least Arturo didn't visit to slow him down.

The following afternoon, just when they had finished chores, Pa noticed that some cows had pushed through a fence. By the time they rounded them up and slid new rails in place, the sun was setting. Nathan slumped on the kitchen steps. His father would use him to get the whole farm in shape before they went, he was sure.

Just as Nathan stood to go into the house, Arturo strolled up. "Hey, farmer boy, you see anything different about me?"

Nathan stared. Arturo's hair had been sheared to within a half-inch of his head, and he was wearing the strap overalls. "Poppa did it for me— he said it's good for summer. Momma doesn't like it."

"You look great!" Nathan said. "Do you want to play mumblety-peg?"

"This time I'll win."

Nathan tried to steer Arturo away from Pa, but Pa spotted him. Pa only grunted. Nathan was so happy with the change in Arturo he didn't even care when he had to pull the matchstick from the ground with his teeth.

The next afternoon Nathan asked Pa, "When do you think we'll be going to White Valley?"

Pa didn't look at him. "The wheel's loose on the

wagon, Nathan. . . . I can't ever seem to get caught up."

"Aw, Pa," Nathan said. "You never take a minute off anymore."

Pa eyed him. "I never felt so pushed before."

Nathan scowled.

That evening he marched Arturo right past Pa to practice target shooting with the slingshot. Later, when they came to the kitchen porch, Nathan saw Pa's *Gazette* folded on the bench where he'd left it. Nathan opened it to show Arturo an article about baseball.

"You know baseball? Look here—this article is about a pitcher right from this county."

He noticed that Arturo ducked his head when he handed him the paper.

"What's the matter? Don't you like baseball?"

Arturo still didn't look at him. "I can't read so good. Momma wants to send me to school, but I must work. She says maybe soon, but I try to teach myself now. You read me this?"

They sat together on the steps, holding the paper, as Nathan read aloud, "Gallatin County Native Pitches No-hitter." Arturo stared at him as if he were doing something wonderful.

Raising his voice, Nathan read clear down the news column without stumbling over a single word.

"There," Nathan said. "You know what? I'll teach you how to read. How would you like that?"

Arturo nodded.

Nathan and Arturo sounded out words from the newspaper awhile. Then Nathan bolted into the house and came back with his *McGuffey Readers*. Ma had ordered them so he would have books of his own to practice reading. He showed Arturo the alphabet in a reader and a story about Frank and Jim and how they cared for their horse. Arturo repeated letters and words after Nathan until the light was gone; and then he ran home in the darkness.

The next evening, when Pa had again put off going to White Valley, Nathan sat Arturo on the porch and brought out his readers, ink, paper, and a pen. Nathan opened a new reader to a story about Henry, a boy who shined boots. Arturo kept stumbling over words, even though Nathan sounded them out. Arturo closed the book and hung his head. "I like the one about the horse."

"But we read that one," Nathan said. "Henry's story is better. If you'd just listen to me, you'd learn the words."

Arturo sounded unhappy. "I want to read the one about the horse."

Nathan handed him the reader from the previous day and huffed, "Here, then. But the horse story is for little kids. American boys our age can read about Henry."

Arturo stared at him. "But I'm not—"

Nathan shoved the book to him. "Just read so you'll learn."

Arturo stumbled over the words in the horse story. Nathan understood why his schoolteacher got angry when kids didn't master their lessons. Looking over Arturo's shoulder, Nathan read the piece aloud quickly. He felt as proud as when he did a lesson better than any other student.

Arturo pulled away and slammed the book. "I cannot do that—"

"If you want to learn, you'll do what I say." Nathan spread the papers, opened the inkwell, and handed Arturo the pen. "Write the alphabet and pronounce each letter."

His jaw set, Arturo bent to the task. He really labored at making his letters. He held the pen so tightly that his fingers went red and the black ink spattered on the page. When he was finished, Nathan asked him to write the alphabet again, even though Arturo gave him a surly look.

Before he could resume writing, Ma appeared with slices of strawberry pie and tall glasses of milk. "I thought you two might enjoy this after sitting still so long."

Finally, Arturo grinned. He showed off his

sheets of smeary letters and then devoured his pie. He quickly accepted the offer of another piece. He looked at Ma and sighed, "I never before eat pie like this."

"I have never eaten pie this good," Nathan corrected. "And don't gobble so fast. I'm still eating my first piece."

Arturo's eyes flared with defiance.

Ma raised an eyebrow at Nathan. He announced that Arturo had had enough schooling for the evening. But Arturo bolted the last of the pie and left anyway.

Ma asked Nathan to stay with her and help with the dishes. As they cleaned up, Ma said, "I think with that haircut and in those overalls Arturo looks skinnier than ever. Do you think it's because he works so hard?"

"I think he looks a lot better than he did. I work hard, too, Ma. He's like me."

"But your bones don't stick out everywhere. And look at yourself—you're already outgrowing your overalls again. Maybe it's because he's underground all day. I read that years ago a law was passed to keep boys like Arturo from working in the mines, but nobody pays any attention to it."

"But I work every day on the farm. I'll bet he's cooler in the mine than I am working in the sun."

"Nathan, Pa and I have heard it's awful in the

mine, and dangerous, with rocks falling on miners all the time and gases that kill people. I pray no one in my family ever sets foot in one. Do you hear me?"

"Aw, Ma, why would I want to?"

"I'm going to fatten that boy up. I'm sure he's not getting enough to eat at home."

Nathan shrugged. Fattening Arturo up seemed like a good idea—that might make him look even more like an ordinary boy. "He sure seems to like your cooking."

"And, Nathan," his mother added as he started up to bed. "Be kinder to him. Remember, he wants to be your friend, not your pupil."

"But he has to learn so he can fit in. Maybe, Pa will even like him then."

Ma sighed.

The next evening after supper, Nathan didn't even ask Pa when they were going to White Valley—he just walked with Arturo past him. Pa never lifted his eyes from his work. He just mumbled hello.

"Why doesn't your Pa like me?" Arturo asked, sitting among the books and papers.

"You've got to understand—Pa hates any change. And my brother died. . . ." Nathan's chest felt squeezed. "I think he was Pa's favorite."

Arturo looked up from the smoked ham sandwich Ma'd given him. "My family had two babies die—my twin brothers. I understand how your Pa—he hurts."

Nathan didn't bother to correct Arturo's English. He just wanted to do or say something nice—but he couldn't think of anything that would help.

Arturo shrugged. "Some die. Too many, Poppa says. We're lucky to be alive, right?"

Nathan forced up his chin and nodded. Besides, he'd just thought of what to do to make Arturo happy.

After Arturo finished the sandwich, Nathan got out Willie, and they rode bareback together around the pasture. Arturo hooted as they bounced up and down. For a while Ma and Pa watched from the fence. Ma grinned. She had her arm linked in Pa's as if she was holding him in place. Then Nathan saw Mr. Tozzi standing in the shadows of the lane.

"Poppa!" Arturo yelled. "Look at me!"

While Nathan guided Willie toward Mr. Tozzi, Pa pulled away from Ma and strode off. Ma walked to the lane fence to meet Mr. Tozzi. He bowed to her but ducked into the shadows to wait for Arturo as though he didn't want to be a bother. But Ma gave a wave, and he returned it.

On Sunday, Nathan wrapped the walnut box with the arrowheads in a scrap of blanket. He didn't want to scratch the box. He had decided to carry his collection to the pond to show Arturo. He figured Arturo deserved a nice surprise, considering how hard he worked and what he'd lived through. Maybe then they wouldn't drift into talking about dead brothers.

When Nathan walked up, Arturo was lying back, propped on his elbows, with his feet in the water. He gazed at the sky.

"You'll go swimming today," Nathan declared.

"It's just nice to rest here—so beautiful in the sun."

"You are bone-lazy or afraid." Nathan laughed. "Which is it?"

Arturo raised his head. "What do you carry?"

"It's a big surprise. I'll tell you what—you go in the water, and I'll show it to you. It has to do with Indians." He uncovered the box to show its size. The waxed walnut gleamed in the sun.

"About Indians, in the box?" Arturo squirmed. "You can teach me to swim without my head going under the water?"

"You bet!" Nathan set the collection on the grass.

"Okay. I'll try." Arturo was unfastening his overall straps when the bushes rustled. Ma with a picnic, Nathan hoped. Instead, Ben and Pete pushed through the bushes.

"Hey, you two!" Nathan yelled.

From the corner of his eye, Nathan glimpsed Arturo refastening his overall straps. Ben's and Pete's smiles faded. They were staring at Arturo as if he were a water moccasin.

★ TEN ★

*I*t's swell you're here," Nathan said to Ben and Pete. He hustled over to put himself between them and Arturo. "Mr. Hoople told us about you visiting. I've been after Pa to drive over to White Valley, but you know Pa. He's always too busy."

"Well, we're going back to Saltsburg tomorrow," Ben said. "Uncle Shep and Aunt Myrt brought us in the wagon. Your Pa told us where you were." Ben looked heavier, and Pete taller. They were both sunburned and the skin was peeling on their faces and arms.

"Uncle Growl and Aunt Screech," Pete sneered. "They're up at the house jawing with your Pa about hard times."

Ben looked serious. "They only sent for us to help them on their farm. They treat us like slaves."

Nathan nodded. "There's no one to help here, either, but me."

Pete stared around his shoulder. "So who's the squirt?"

Nathan flinched. Arturo had waited in place. "Arthur, come here," Nathan said. "This is Art."

Arturo's lips were set in a thin line, but he didn't correct him. Good, he was smartening up. Pete could be real trouble.

"Ben and Pete are old friends who used to live . . ." Nathan groped for words. He couldn't say where—what if Arturo mentioned that he now lived there? "Nearby," he mumbled.

He felt out of breath.

Ben stuck out his thick hand to Arturo, but Pete knocked it aside. He put his finger on Arturo's chest. "What's your last name?"

"Let's go swimming," Nathan interrupted. "What do you say, Ben?" Maybe that would make Arturo head for home.

"Sure." Ben wiped sweat from his face with a dirty hand. "I'm melting."

Nathan and he skinned down to their drawers, but Pete frowned at Arturo.

Nathan muttered to Arturo, "I'm going to swim. If you don't want to today . . ."

"Who is he, anyway?" Pete demanded.

"Just a new pal—a guy like us," Nathan answered.

"He's no guy like us!" Pete's sneer showed his

73

yellowed teeth. "With hair and skin that color? He's one of those greaseball foreigners."

Ben leaped back. "You mean he's one of those Italians who moved in?"

Nathan kept his voice low and edged toward Pete. "Simmer down now. He comes here every day learning to be a fellow like us. You'll see. He's going to be a real American."

Pete grabbed Arturo by the arm. "Well, then, let's throw him in the pond. Maybe if we scrub the filth off, he'll look like us."

Arturo twisted free. He raised his chin. With his close-clipped hair, his nose looked like a beak. But he scowled at Nathan, not at Pete. "My name is Arturo Tozzi. I never came here to learn to be just like you!"

Nathan reached for him, but Arturo strode off across the meadow.

"Now you know how stupid he is," Pete snickered. He shoved Nathan, toppling him backward into the pond.

"Artur-o Toz-zi. What a moniker!" Ben hooted. He belly-flopped into the pond and grappled with Nathan.

Before he could get free, Pete jumped in. While Ben held Nathan, Pete forced his head under. All went bubbling green. His ears hurt and his lungs burned. Finally, he got away and burst clear of the surface, gagging to empty his throat.

Arturo had gone from the meadow—better that he was out of this. Ben and Pete swam toward Nathan. They wrestled him until his arms and legs hurt so much he begged, "Just let me float a minute."

Ben floated beside him. As Pete crawled out onto the grass, Nathan saw welts on his lower back.

"He just never gives in until Pa licks him," Ben murmured. "I got gumption, but I'm not as ornery as him."

"I know." Nathan glanced at Ben's white bulk. He had plenty of bruises, but Pete had probably given him those.

After they'd floated awhile, Ben looked at Nathan. "Uncle Shep told us the coal company pulled down our house and buildings and used the scraps to make shanties. Is that true?"

"I don't know," Nathan lied. "Everything's just changed."

"I don't want to see," Ben whispered. "That Art-ur-o, where's he live?"

Nathan swallowed hard. "I'm not sure. . . . What's it like living in Saltsburg?"

"Awful. Now I got Pap and Grandpap both on me to get chores done. And Uncle Shep's worse than them. When I grow up, I swear I'm getting a job off the farm."

From the grass Pete shouted, "What's this?" He opened Nathan's box and held up an arrowhead. "Let's see if it'll skip." He fired it into the pond.

"Stop!" Nathan hollered. He couldn't lose the arrowheads, too. He flung himself out of the water and ran at Pete. They went down, knocking over the box and scattering the arrowheads. Pete pounded on him, but Nathan managed to roll him away from the box and back into the pond. Ben got into the scuffle, grappling to hold on to Pete.

Nathan stood up and punched Pete on the chest and shoulders, harder than he'd ever punched anyone. Pete shoved loose from Ben and shouted, "Gotten feisty? Think you're tough enough to take me on?" Pete tried to pin Nathan's hands while jabbing at his head and neck. Nathan kept thumping at him.

"That's enough!" Pa stood beside the pond.

Nathan stumbled back onto the grass. Pete came on with fists raised, but Pa got one hand on Pete and the other on Nathan. "Up to the house now. Ma's fixed something to eat."

Nathan, panting, staggered up the bank. He couldn't look at Pa. He gathered what arrowheads he could. A hinge on the box had been torn loose. Nathan held the box to his chest so Pa wouldn't see. Red-faced, Pa herded them all to the house.

Ma was waiting in the kitchen with Uncle Shep and Aunt Myrt. The table had been set with cold Sunday supper, and Ma blessed the food. Nathan didn't speak. He watched Ben and Pete wolf down Ma's sandwiches and pie. He felt as mean and spiteful as a caged coon. He matched them bite for bite. He grinned only when Pete got cuffed by his uncle for spilling milk all over the cloth. Then, Ben burped and stopped the grownups' talk.

Uncle Shep hustled the boys out right after supper. Neither Ben nor Pete raised a hand in farewell. When their wagon rolled out of the yard, Pa eyed Nathan. "Ben and Pete act like roughnecks. All along I thought they were decent fellows." His voice sounded blaming.

Nathan hung his head. He hadn't stuck up for Arturo when he should have, and then he'd gone wild, wanting to beat Pete up. His face burned. "They're fellows—like me, I guess," he muttered.

Ma looked alarmed.

"Well, you're not going to start acting like them, Nathan," Pa said.

Nathan nodded.

As he stumbled up the steps to bed, he wondered why he'd ever missed Ben and Pete at all. He felt more alone than ever.

ELEVEN

The next morning Nathan waited beside the lane. The miners came striding two and three together in their dark jackets and pants and their caps with brass lamps. Nathan noticed there were still none among them as young as Arturo. One of the passing miners pointed at him, and the others looked alert. The miner taunted, "Look. He acts nice. He don't like being hung from his fence." The others, who heard, laughed.

Nathan stood his ground. Farther up the line, Arturo walked between his poppa and Ernesto.

"Hey," Nathan called and raised his hand.

Arturo didn't so much as look. Mr. Tozzi nodded to Nathan. Ernesto scowled from under his dark eyebrows.

That evening Nathan waited as the miners dragged home, straggling up the lane. Ernesto passed silently, a bit stooped, maybe not even see-ing him. Arturo trailed along with his father. Mr. Tozzi stepped ahead, and Nathan ran over and said, "Arturo, be sure to come later."

Arturo shook his head.

"Ben and Pete are gone."

Arturo kept walking and mumbled, "Why would I want to be with you, a farmer boy?"

Nathan stopped. He stood alone in the lane and stared after the miners.

The next day Nathan didn't go near the lane. At nightfall he sat on the kitchen steps, his head supported by his hands. Ma brought him some fresh-baked oatmeal cookies.

"Is Arturo stopping tonight?" she asked.

"I don't know."

"He was with you at the pond on Sunday. With Ben and Pete there—something happened, didn't it?"

The cookie in his mouth tasted like sawdust. "It's all Ben and Pete's fault. If they hadn't been so mean, I wouldn't have said anything, and Arturo wouldn't have gotten upset." He knew that wasn't all of it. Why didn't any scheme of his work out? His throat knotted around the cookie, and he stammered, "All I said was I was teaching Arturo how to be a regular guy like us. He got real mad. Now he won't even stop to talk."

Ma put her hand on Nathan's shoulder. "I warned you not to act uppity—that he didn't want to be your pupil."

"I thought he had to learn—"

"If you really want to see him, you may have to go to his house and apologize. Treat him like a real friend."

He'd have to visit the hollow again—all that muck and smell—and be among the miners. He'd even have to go inside Arturo's house. Mr. and Mrs. Tozzi would let him in, but how would Ernesto act—and Arturo?

Nathan didn't speak, and Ma left him.

The next few days, morning and evening, he just hid in the spruce trees by the lane, spying. On Saturday evening he picked a handful of young crab apples. He'd make Arturo stop.

The miners came up the lane slowly. In their midst Ernesto and some other miners were carrying a litter. Mr. Tozzi lay on it with one arm wrapped in a sling. His face looked gray, and he was gritting his teeth. Arturo walked beside him and held his poppa's good hand.

Dropping the apples, Nathan dashed out. "What happened? He didn't get beat up, did he?"

"He was in a cave-in," a nearby miner answered.

Arturo frowned. "What do you care, farmer boy?"

"Maybe I can help."

"We don't want help from people like you," Arturo spat out. He struggled on, but Nathan saw him wipe at his eyes with a fist.

"Nathan." Pa stepped out from the trees. "You'd better come with me."

Nathan hesitated, watching the miners go, but then followed Pa to the livery shed. Pa started mending Willie's halter before he spoke. "Are you sure you want a fellow like that for a friend?"

Nathan wanted to yell "Yes!" but Pa would only be contrary. Instead, he kicked at a bale of straw. "He's not fit company for me, right?"

Pa kept working on the harness. "He's different." Bending his head over the harness, he muttered, "Right now, we just don't need more difficulties."

"What about Ben and Pete, Pa?" Nathan tried to keep his voice quiet. "They're the same as me— but they're roughnecks. I shouldn't be with them, either, right?"

Pa nodded. "I think it's the way Pap Robinson is handling those two."

"That leaves you and me," Nathan said. "Can we go fishing tomorrow?"

His father flushed. "Don't you understand I have to work to save this farm? I was hoping to trade help for the haying, at least, with Shep Robinson and the farmers in White Valley, but most of them are only praying the coal vein stretches that far so they can sell their land." His eyes darkened. "And you know we've been dealing with other troubles besides."

"Arturo's father was hurt in the mine, but he isn't looking for anybody's help." Nathan bolted from the door of the livery shed and ran across the yard to the house. He escaped Ma, who called from the kitchen, "Now what, Nathan?"

Ma didn't climb the stairs after him. When Pa came in, he didn't come up, either. Nathan flopped on the bed with his arrowhead collection. Only thirty-six arrowheads remained. He tried to push the bent hinge of the box back into place. If this was about who was fit company, Arturo would win hands down. But Arturo was acting ornery. Nathan punched his pillow. He had turned him ornery.

The next morning Pa went to church with Nathan and his mother but moped up the aisle. Nathan was feeling pretty down himself when only the same crew attended Sunday school. His father fidgeted beside him all through Reverend McMurty's sermon, and then came outside as gray-faced as Mr. Tozzi had been on his stretcher. Ma touched Pa's arm and said, "Aren't you feeling more comforted now?"

Pa shrugged and looked at Nathan. "If I get my work done, and Nathan and I get to run Chimer, that'll help me feel better."

Nathan got into the buggy between his parents and stared forward. He had to believe Pa meant well. Still, he wouldn't hold his breath waiting for Pa to yell, "Let Chimer loose."

Later, Nathan sat by the lane, his boots at his side, waiting for his father. The shadows showed it was going on four. When they'd reached the farm, Pa had been convinced a storm was coming. The clouds were mounting to the west, and soon Pa was pounding tin patches on the livery shed roof. When Nathan offered to climb up with him, Pa had just sighed. "Leaks are bad enough. I can't have you falling and breaking your neck."

Now Nathan squeezed his eyes shut. Pa had become such an old fusspot. If Harry were still alive, would both of them be up on the roof helping Pa? Or would they just be running the afternoon away in the yard? He opened his eyes. He wasn't wasting the afternoon playing chase with "What if?" He wished Arturo would walk along the lane.

But only a hot wind came past, rustling the trees and whirling the dust. He might as well wish that Pa would show up with Chimer.

Nathan stood, shoved his feet in his boots, and

headed toward shanty hollow. Arturo had to understand he'd just blurted the wrong words. Nathan forced his feet over the crest of the hill through the thick dust.

And there was Arturo, trudging halfway up the hill toward him. Nathan stopped and waved, waiting for him to come.

Arturo came faster. His hair was growing in. He was wearing a shirt, his work pants, and boots. He had his head and shoulders back, and he was looking as mean as Ernesto. He steamed right past Nathan.

"Hey, wait," Nathan said. "I thought we . . ."

Arturo kept walking. "I told you—we don't talk."

Nathan caught up with him. "I didn't mean to treat you bad. Those guys are tough. Their house stood where you live. I was scared of what they'd do when they found out, and I just said the wrong words trying to protect you, and if you thought I was acting better than you, I didn't mean it."

Arturo snorted.

"Where are you headed now?" Nathan asked. "I'll come with you."

Arturo stopped and glared. "You don't want to go where I do. Ernesto says you treat me worse than a dog. I visit your house. You don't visit mine. You think I don't notice? Ernesto is right about all of you. You don't want to know Arturo Tozzi. Go to your animals and your big brick house, farmer." He strode down the lane.

Nathan halted. How much humble pie was he going to have to eat? He deserved to eat a little, he guessed, and it probably wouldn't choke him.

★ TWELVE ★

*W*ait! I'm coming with you." Nathan was panting as he caught up with Arturo. "Where are we headed?"

Arturo didn't answer. He walked out of the lane and turned right on the main road toward town. The clouds from the west had covered the sun, but the gusts of wind were still hot.

No wagons traveled past. Alongside the road the ribbons of iron rails led toward town. Coal cars lined the tracks near the mine yard, but no engine steamed nearby. The town lay silent, except for his and Arturo's thudding boots and heavy breathing.

A tan-and-white hound slunk across their path as they approached Main Street. The buildings loomed over them, the frames for two more new ones jutting among them. "I don't think this beats walking in our woods," Nathan muttered. "Do you want to head there?"

Arturo frowned. At the depot he stopped a second to look around. Nathan saw Mr. Hoople in the shed at the end of the platform chatting with a switchman. Did Mr. Hoople ever go home anymore, Nathan wondered, or did he just meet trains?

Arturo walked up the middle of Main Street, gazing from side to side. Ahead, Mr. Mueller sat on a rocker on the front porch of his store. His eyes widened and he leaned forward. "Nathan, is that you? Who is that you're walking with? You'd better come right here, boy."

Arturo clenched his fists, lowered his head, and just kept walking.

Nathan trotted to stay beside him. "Don't pay any attention. He doesn't mean anything. He thinks he's the boss of the whole town. His daughters treat me the same way. They're getting money now, and it's going to their heads."

"Money from the likes of us," Arturo said.

As they turned the corner, Nathan heard Mr. Mueller yell, "I'm telling your pa." Nathan clenched his own fists and followed Arturo up the hill.

Nathan saw that the company had built more row houses, perched on the hillside on stone pilings. Women on their steps watched their playing infants. Nathan smelled the odor of simmering onion, garlic, and tomato. He had to admit it made his mouth water.

Arturo stared in every open door.

"Who are you looking for?" Nathan asked.

Without answering, Arturo mounted the plank walk and moved faster.

Nathan kept pace as they passed a new white-washed plank building. A sign identified it as the payroll office. "You're as stubborn as a tick on a hound's belly," Nathan said, "but I can be, too."

He could hear voices ahead. He followed Arturo right into the center of a cluster of shanties near another new building, a three-story box. Nathan slowed for a moment. A sign on the porch advertised the place as Sichena's Boardinghouse. His village had become all matchstick buildings, jumbled over hillsides, like one of those Wild West boomtowns he'd read about in school.

The boardinghouse porch and yard were packed with men and even boys, some just a little older than Arturo. A few blond, ruddy-faced men gestured and talked in a language that didn't sound like Italian. Mr. Hoople had been right—other foreigners had arrived. This was some sort of miners' meeting.

Arturo pushed on, weaving among the men, and Nathan plowed after him until he reached the steps of the boardinghouse. Nathan spied Ernesto on the porch and halted as Arturo disappeared among the crowd.

The men around Nathan suddenly stopped talking and eyed him. He stared back, feeling like a fox surrounded by hounds. Well, he wasn't going to run away.

Arturo finally appeared beside Ernesto, who looked surprised. Arturo grabbed hold of his brother's shirtfront and said, "*Per favore*, Ernesto. *Ritorni a casa!*"

The men snickered.

"*Basta!* Enough, little one!" Ernesto shouted.

Arturo clung to his brother's shirt, but Ernesto pulled free of him and lifted him into the air. He swaggered about with him and then, grabbing his ankles, suspended Arturo over the porch railing.

Arturo howled, and the men laughed. Ernesto raised and lowered him by the ankles, but kept his head and hands inches from the trampled ground.

Nathan pushed forward. How could Arturo's brother bully him in front of all these men?

"Let him go!" Nathan cried. He braced Arturo's shoulders. When Ernesto released his grip, Nathan helped Arturo somersault to his feet. Ernesto threw back his head and laughed.

Arturo pushed Nathan aside and shook his fists at Ernesto, but he sounded as if he was pleading with him. "Ernesto, *ritorni a casa. Subito.*"

Ernesto folded his arms and turned his back on him.

Arturo shoved his way through the men and headed down the hill. Nathan followed. "What were you asking your brother?" he asked.

Arturo started to run.

Nathan grabbed his arm. "Whoa! I helped you like you helped me when he put me on the fence post. Remember? So tell me what's wrong."

Arturo smacked his fist into his palm. "He must come home. Now. Ernesto is a bullhead. He is so big he thinks he can handle everything, but he always gets into trouble. Shale in the mine fell and hurt my poppa. Ernesto stirs up others to shut the mine with a strike. He wants to bring in the union. If the men strike, we will lose our jobs and houses."

Nathan had read about trouble from strikes in the *Gazette*. He broke in, "But if he knows that, why—"

"He thinks he's right—he's a bullhead. He did this before in Connellsville. The owners marked Ernesto out. That's why Poppa brought us to start over at this new mine. We are close to becoming citizens, and Momma's afraid Ernesto will be arrested. The government will send him back to Italy. He will never be a citizen, and we won't have him or his wages. Momma and Teresa will blame me if I don't bring him home!" He shut up as if he was embarrassed and walked away fast.

Nathan kept pace with him as they passed the

stores on Main Street. Mr. Mueller had vanished indoors. Thunder rumbled and the gusting wind blew grit that stung his eyes. He knew how Arturo felt—Ma and Pa had sent him enough times to keep Harry out of trouble. Nathan shook his head. As if Arturo's family didn't have enough to worry about with Mr. Tozzi hurt and not able to work.

"How's your poppa?" Nathan asked.

"What do you care?"

"What do you mean? I stayed with you, didn't I?"

"Now you see how Tozzis carry on and fight. You can go back to your father and tell all about us."

"We argue plenty, too," Nathan said quietly. "Pa and me—you bet." He frowned. If that were true, then maybe he could tell Pa what he really felt.

Arturo turned down a side road and crossed the rail tracks. Nathan stayed on his heels. They stopped beside the locked gates of the mine yard. Rain spattered the ground.

"You think you're brave," Arturo yelled above the wind. "You don't dare go where I work."

"You think I wouldn't?" Nathan stared into Arturo's face. His back tingled the way it had when Harry and Pete had pulled him up into a giant sycamore and nagged him into climbing alone into higher branches. But this wasn't just some crazy challenge. He was being asked to go where Arturo worked every day. Nathan did want to see inside the mine that had changed everything. But if Pa ever knew, he'd strap him, for sure.

Nathan looked along the road and into the mine yard. No one was about. The rain pattered harder. "Some days I've seen a watchman. Where is he?"

"I saw him on the porch with Ernesto," Arturo answered. Then he smirked. "You ready?"

"Let's go," Nathan said.

★ THIRTEEN ★

*A*rturo pushed at the flimsy gates. The chain held, but the gates separated eleven, maybe twelve, inches. Arturo shoved his head and shoulders into the space and then forced his whole body through. "You coming, farmer boy?"

Nathan followed. He twisted between the gates, scraping the side of his head and his bare arms, and got into the yard. Arturo looked surprised but still managed to sneer. The rails that led into the dark mine glistened in the quickening rain. Nathan shivered. He asked, "What are we waiting for?"

Arturo marched toward a plank-sided building near the mine entrance. As he followed, Nathan stumbled over the shale and coal scattered about the yard. He hoped a guard would jump from somewhere and grab them.

Arturo held the door open, his eyes daring Nathan to enter. Nathan walked ahead and into the one-room shed. In the light from the door, he could make out the stained enamel washbasins that lined one side of the room. On the other side, a few miners' hats lay piled on a shelf. Arturo pulled down two of them. He grabbed two tiny lamps. He checked the oil and the wicks, and clipped a lamp to each hat, above the bill. Arturo put one on his head and shoved the other into Nathan's hands. "Wear it if you want to see."

Nathan inspected the grimy cap and its little lamp.

"Maybe you don't want to put it on."

Well, as Ben always said, *In for a penny, in for a whole greenback.* Nathan's heart pounded, but he jammed the cap on his head. He smelled the sweat that stained it.

From a nail by the door Arturo snatched a wire-handled lamp, which held a glass tube. Nathan marched with him back into the yard, which now seemed a lot grayer, wetter, and emptier than it had earlier. Nathan didn't hesitate as they strode past the mine cars. The rain spattered into them. Nathan felt drops running on his bare arms and down his back under his overalls.

With his head lowered, Arturo walked along the tracks, stepping from tie to tie. The mine entrance gaped in front of them. It was a black hole barely six feet high and six feet wide. Nathan had seen that some miners had to bend to enter it and that a mule and a cart just barely seemed to fit.

Arturo marched toward the hole. Nathan planted his boots exactly where Arturo stepped. Arturo trotted inside.

The mine opening breathed the odor of dank earth into Nathan's face. He choked. His legs started to shake, but he went in. The mine air chilled his wet skin, and a sulfur smell bit into his nose and throat. He heard water trickling somewhere deep inside the tunnel. He stopped. Hadn't he done it? Hadn't he gone far enough?

In the shadowy entrance, Arturo snickered. Nathan forced a laugh. It sounded like a gag.

"Farmer boy is so brave," Arturo taunted.

"I'm as brave as you," Nathan said.

Arturo set the little lamp on the track. Taking matches from his pocket, he lit the lamp and held it before Nathan's face. The flame in the glass cylinder burned white and steady.

"The gases in a mine—they can kill," Arturo said. "Sometimes they knock out miners. If no one comes along and drags them to fresh air, they die. Sometimes the gases explode. This safety lamp—if it glows brighter, then the gas is a danger. Maybe this is far enough for you? You won't go into the mine?"

This was crazier than any dare he'd ever accepted

from Pete or Harry. "If you can go, I can, too," he answered.

Arturo struck another match and lit the lamp on his own hat and then on Nathan's. The flames glowed yellow. Arturo lifted the lamp with the glass cylinder and stepped off down the track.

Nathan pushed himself forward. The rails gleamed in the lamplight, but he could only see a few feet into the blackness. The space seemed to narrow inside. The rock roof loomed just inches over his head, and he felt he could almost touch both sides of the tunnel at once. The miners must have to crouch the whole way in, he thought. The mule and cart must just scrape through.

Nathan stumbled on loose coal underfoot. Water trickled from the walls and ran across the tracks. He felt the wet soaking through his boots, chilling his feet.

Arturo walked still deeper into the tunnel. Nathan told himself this was better than the cave Pete had once dragged him and Ben into—and he had lived through that. These oil lamps showed more than the candles they'd had then. And the mine was shored up with timbers. But Pete, Ben, and he had gone only into the front part of the cave, still warmed by the sun. And the cave didn't hold dangerous gases—that he knew of.

Arturo held the lamp high. It didn't flicker, and

in the glow Nathan could see rooms off the main tunnel. The walls and floor glistened. The coal seemed to sparkle. Arturo shone his lamp on an open wooden door and a low bench beside it. "Most times I sit here when I don't work with Poppa and Ernesto. This is a trap," he said. "I am responsible to keep it shut. Aboveground in the ventilator shack a fan blows clean air to where the miners dig—no gas collects. Only when the mules bring out the coal do I open the trap. Do you go out now, or do you want to see how we dig the coal?"

Nathan tried to keep his voice steady. "Since I'm here, show me."

As they passed by, he stared at the little bench where Arturo sat in the darkness. How did he stay here twelve minutes, let alone twelve hours a day?

Arturo still held the wire-handled lamp high as he edged into a chamber. Nathan now shivered in the damp cold. He followed Arturo, watching the lamp's steady flame. The walls of coal shimmered in the lamplight. "The miners dig coal from the bottom of the wall. They pound in rods to make holes for blasting powder. Then they blast the wall of coal down. They break it up and shovel it into cars. The mules haul it out to be weighed at the tipple. When I help Poppa and Ernesto, I throw the coal into our car."

Nathan couldn't see Arturo's face. The harshness, though, had left his voice. "How did your father get hurt?"

"Poppa and Ernesto hid when the powder went off. Shale fell from the roof onto Poppa. The men want to leave more coal pillars to hold up the roof. The company says the timbers we use are enough. But they're wrong. The rock fell on Poppa. The company says if we use more timbers, we must pay for them."

Nathan flashed his light toward Arturo's face. The shadows made Arturo's eyes and cheeks look sunken, his face sad.

"It's hard to work down here," Nathan said.

"It's hard, but aboveground is harder for us." The meanness was back in his voice. "Nobody wants us in this country—only to work in the mines."

"How far does the mine go?" If he could keep Arturo talking, the edge might disappear again.

"Not so far yet, since it's new. The gas is not bad in this mine. The old mine we worked was dug out for miles and was very deep. Maybe you want a job in this mine, like me?" he asked, sounding sour again. "Ernesto can get a job for you—earn you fifty cents a day."

Nathan almost shouted "Not me!" Instead, he held his tongue. But the Tozzis and the others had to work here. If the farm failed, would Pa and he end up someplace like this or in a mill?

A critter scurried past. The dark shape ran over his boot. He jumped back. Other shapes rushed along the track. "What's that?"

"Rats," Arturo answered. "We feed them. If you have no food, maybe they take a bite out of you. Are you ready to run out of the mine yet?"

"No," Nathan mumbled. "If you can take it, so can I."

But Arturo turned away. "You can stay. I'm going now. I must tell Momma I cannot bring Ernesto home." He started back up the track at a fast pace.

Crouching, Nathan followed as fast as he could in the darkness. He was certain that with every step he'd stumble on a rat. Arturo had gotten far ahead. Nathan could barely see him. In spite of the cold, sweat soaked his back. Was Arturo really trying to leave him? No, Arturo wasn't like that. Nathan caught up to him.

Within a few hundred yards, Nathan could make out dim light. With every stride, it grew. He hustled forward, surprised that the trip out seemed so short.

Just inside the mine entry he stopped, gulping fresh air. Arturo must know he'd been scared. Nathan didn't care. He'd stayed with him, hadn't he—gone to where he worked?

The rain poured, but Nathan plunged into the

wet anyway. For a second he threw back his face and let the rain pelt him and stream down his body. The water felt warm. He let it trickle from his face into his mouth. Then he followed Arturo to the building to return the hats and lamps. Without a word, the two boys splashed across the mine yard, squeezed out the gate, and slogged through mud.

Nathan kept pace with Arturo down the main road and into the lane. Arturo kept his head and shoulders bent forward, as if he were carrying a bundle on his back. Nathan waited for him to talk, but he didn't.

When they reached the farm, Nathan grabbed Arturo's arm and stopped him. "Okay. I'm sorry. I mean it. I didn't know anything before. You've got a lot of grit to work in the mine. I don't think I could do it. Let's go in and warm up. After, if you want, I'll go with you to your family and tell how Ernesto wouldn't listen to you."

Arturo glanced at him. There was a flicker of his old grin.

"Nathan! Get in the house!" Pa yelled from the kitchen porch.

The grin vanished and Arturo stiffened. "Listen to your pa, farmer boy. He does not want you with an Italian miner." He stepped off, his back straight, his fists out in front. He looked like Ernesto.

"But that's Pa, not me," Nathan said. And he was going to have to make that clear to Pa—and hope he didn't get a strapping for it.

★ FOURTEEN ★

"Don't you dare defend those immigrant miners to me," Pa said, his voice rising.

Ma banged a skillet on the hot stove. Nathan knew she wouldn't cross Pa in front of him, but the clang interrupted Pa. "Why not hear what Nathan has to say?"

Nathan stood his ground, water streaming off him onto the kitchen floor. "I'm not defending all the miners. I only know Arturo." His voice quavered, but he forced the words out. "I like to be with him. He's got plenty of gumption, and he isn't mean like Pete and Ben."

Pa's face reddened. He ran his hands through his blond hair. "I can't believe you. Those miners are ruining the whole valley, and our lives with it. I'm trying to protect you."

Ma banged the skillet again.

Nathan's heart pounded, but he kept his voice

soft. "Arturo and his family are only working in the mine to stay alive. They didn't open it, Pa."

"What do we do but work to stay alive? And their coming here has just about ruined us."

"Pa, they have it harder than we do. They don't own anything at all. They have to work all day underground." He finally blurted out, "Pa, they're like us. Arturo's family even had babies that died—two of them. But, Pa, they don't act like they want to die, too."

His father's head snapped back. Nathan wished he'd held his tongue.

"Nathan's only trying to say he wants Arturo as a friend," Ma said quickly. "Arturo's a good boy, from decent people."

Nathan could see the grieving in Pa's eyes and touched his arm.

Pa suddenly clasped Nathan in a hug. Nathan folded against him for an instant. But this wasn't a bear hug that was going to end up with them both hooting with laughter. It was a hug filled with pain and worry—meant to hem him in. Nathan stiffened, and Pa released him.

Pa's eyes were sad, but that jaw of his was set and he said, "That's enough talk, Nathan. You're not allowed to run with him or any of them. All of a sudden, you're frisking like some wild colt. Well, I won't let you hurt yourself. Until you're tamed a bit, you're allowed outside only to do chores. Now get to your room."

His mother shut her eyes but nodded in agreement with Pa. Nathan marched slowly up the stairs like a prisoner. He stood in his wet overalls by the window in his bedroom. The rain poured from clouds that seemed to eddy around the trees and against the panes. From downstairs, he heard Ma and Pa continuing to disagree. Nathan couldn't make out the words. He could hear Pa's voice, complaining and mournful—and Ma's, sweet and soothing. Ma never gave up when she knew she was right. She never quit, no matter what.

Later, his father marched through the doorway and handed him a tray full of supper. Ma had probably sent him so he and Pa could talk. Pa set the tray on the desk.

"I'm sorry if what I said hurt you," Nathan said.

Pa shook his head. "For your own good, you just do what I tell you."

"But, Pa, I'm not a tyke anymore. I'm growing and—"

Pa eyed him up and down and nodded as if he was seeing that. But without another word, he went out the door.

Nathan picked at his food. Well, he'd tried. He guessed that he could just sneak off to see Arturo. But that would be acting like Harry or Pete, and he knew already what that could bring. Maybe he ought to get some of Ma's attitude—peaceful and sure—just working like she believed things were going to get better. Nathan sighed. More than likely, he'd just end up trapped on this farm, struggling to keep it from falling to pieces, while Pa got worse.

The next two days his father kept a close watch on him. Nathan didn't even see the miners heading to work because he didn't dare leave his milking stool. He might as well be tethered. Wild colt? He felt more like a dumb mule. But he went through all his paces, doing every chore Pa asked. At dusk Pa even kept him in the barn, so he didn't see Arturo pass toward home. All Nathan wanted was a word with him at the fence.

It poured again late Wednesday. Nathan sat in his room, idly fooling with the slingshot that Arturo had given him. Through his window he glimpsed Arturo and Ernesto wading up the muddy lane under the bent trees. Their father wasn't with them—he must have really been injured.

Nathan raised the window and called, "Arturo." The rushing water and wind probably carried his call away, because Arturo never looked up. Nathan didn't dare shout.

On Thursday, since the gray sky still dripped, Pa and he cleaned the livery shed together and then brushed Willie and Star. Nathan worked extra hard, hoping Pa would notice. "Nice job," Pa managed, but that stern jaw told Nathan he had no intention of letting him go.

They mended fence all afternoon in a cold drizzle. When every post and rail was set to Pa's satisfaction, he laid a hand on Nathan's shoulder. "I know you're angry, but you work real hard. And you never stop."

Those words eased the aches in Nathan's arms and legs, and he grinned. Pa almost managed a grin back, but then the evening mine whistle blew and he looked away, as if trying to ignore it and the soreness between them.

Nathan pleaded, "Just let me walk to the hollow with him."

Pa stared at the puddles in the front yard. "Nathan, I know you're growing. And the time is coming when you'll make your own decisions. But for now I think it's better if we keep to our own kind."

"Arturo is a boy like me, Pa."

His father didn't answer. He clenched his teeth and stared at the rain.

Nathan splashed off toward the kitchen. "Aw, Ma," he complained as he came into the house, "I have to get loose. I have to explain to Arturo. He'll think I settled on keeping away."

Ma handed him a laundered flour sack to dry himself. "I've been working on Pa. So much has gone wrong, nothing feels safe to him. And he worries too much about keeping you safe." She hugged Nathan. "He's a good man. He'll get all this unstuck from his craw, and he'll come around. You'll see."

When, Nathan wondered. If it took too long, Arturo would never speak to him again. As far as he could tell, Pa had a chunk so big caught in his craw, it might never get loose. And Pa's constant worrying had a way of seeping into him, like the rain through the tiniest chink in the roof.

★ FIFTEEN ★

*T*he sun finally burned through the clouds on Friday. Pa had asked Nathan to help hoe weeds that were sprouting in the vegetable patch. Nathan paused to watch his father. He was hoeing the weeds as if they were demons and he would root out every one. Pa nodded for Nathan to get on with it—the trainer with his slow-witted mule.

All morning Nathan had kept pace, and he wasn't going to quit now. He wielded his hoe again with energy. Well, he wouldn't stop asking to get free, no matter how long it took. Once he got to the hollow, Arturo could be lured into talking, Nathan was sure of it. He would show the box of arrowheads to him.

The sun warmed Nathan's shoulders as he worked. The smell in the air made his mouth water—Ma's bread was baking. Someday, when he got free, he'd take a hunk to eat with Arturo.

Arturo couldn't resist Ma's cooking for long. Nathan, leaning on his hoe and dreaming of a warm piece slathered in butter, suddenly noticed that the birds had fallen silent. He gazed around.

The mine whistle screamed.

Pa stopped hoeing, and Ma came out onto the kitchen porch. Nathan saw the crows lift from the cornfields and circle. Ma covered her ears. The whistle shrilled until its steam ran out. Nathan dropped his hoe and raced toward the fence, his head throbbing. He stared up and down the lane. Ma and Pa rushed up behind him.

Over the crest of the muddy lane women and children were running full speed toward the mine. Wild-eyed and pale-faced, they carried crying babies with them.

The whistle built steam and shrilled again. Nathan felt the noise tearing into him.

Nathan saw Mr. Tozzi coming from his home, with Arturo's momma and Teresa next to him. Mr. Tozzi's arm was still in a sling, and his face was white and twisted with the effort of walking.

"Mr. Tozzi!" Nathan called. "What's happened?"

"An accident—in the mine!" a small boy running past shouted.

Mrs. Tozzi brought up the bottom of her apron to wipe her eyes. Arturo's family glanced toward

Nathan but kept heading toward the mine, holding on to each other.

He turned from the fence to face Pa. Nathan set his jaw and looked him right in the eyes. "I have to go."

Pa didn't look so in charge anymore. He chewed the inside of his cheek. His eyes wouldn't meet Nathan's. They looked sad, like the eyes of the injured fox pup Pete had caged over a year ago. It had paced and panted with worried eyes. Then it had died. "Better to stay here," Pa finally said. "This isn't our problem. It's theirs. You don't know what you could be getting into. You don't have to go looking for trouble. It must be clear by now that soon enough trouble comes looking for you."

"People need help, Pa," Nathan said. Why couldn't he understand? Pa wasn't being caged—he was caging himself. "The Tozzis have two sons in the mine. They've already lost two babies."

His mother plucked at his father's arm. "David, he's right."

Pa's mouth set in a straight line. "You care what happens to them that much?"

Nathan looked down the lane. He wanted to know what was going on, to be there when Arturo, even Ernesto, came out of the hole in the earth. But what if they were injured or trapped? What nightmare was happening in that mine? Nathan turned back to Pa. From his father's strained face Nathan could tell he had already thought of all that, but he hadn't said anything. Nathan knew he could just stay with Pa and play it safe—and let Pa put him in a cage, too. "I have to go," Nathan repeated.

Pa blinked. He looked as if he were about to reach out and grab Nathan, but he kept his hands at his side. "All right, Nathan," Pa said. "Maybe it's time you learn for yourself." He turned away.

Nathan looked at Ma. She nodded. He took a breath, clambered through the fence, and took off running.

When Nathan reached the mine yard, he saw that most of the people in town were there—miners' wives and children, ancient grandparents, Mr. Hoople, the lumbermen, carpenters, railroad workers, farmers.

The awful whistle finally ceased. People's voices rose. Nathan could hear the fear in all the jabbering. He squirmed forward. The flimsy gates to the mine yard had been closed, and people waited before them. Where were the Tozzis? Was Arturo with them? Then, farther along the fence line, he saw Mr. and Mrs. Tozzi—without Arturo or Ernesto.

The mine yard, the mine entrance, and the buildings looked undamaged. A man was dragging away a braying, kicking mule. Yard workers hovered near the dark entry. That hole of a mine—had gases somehow exploded? But Arturo had told him this new mine didn't have a lot of the bad gases.

Then Nathan could see miners walking out of the mine on the gleaming tracks. Some in the yard whistled and clapped. Nathan clung to the fence. Arturo wasn't with them. Other miners struggled out of the mine entrance. Some were being carried on planks. Everyone around Nathan became silent.

Miners brought out a mule-drawn mine car. In it were men who had been laid over the coal. People in the crowd moaned. The yard workers just plucked the injured men from the car and put them on the muddy ground like pieces of wood. A yard worker swung open the gates, and people began spilling into the yard. Nathan pushed through the gate. Workers were carrying out other men. Was Arturo there? He couldn't see because of the people. He tried to get closer to the miners who were laid out on the ground, but yard workers were shouting and pushing people back.

Nathan listened for English words among the shouts of Italian. "Give them air! Get back! They're hurt—they need air to breathe." Another yardman shouted to the townspeople, "The roof fell in a new shaft—may have been an explosion.

112

But there's no fire yet. Some men are trapped beyond the fall."

Through the jostling crowd, Nathan saw injured miners being lifted onto a flatbed wagon that was hitched to a pair of mules. The driver moved the wagon toward the gate, but people jammed around, trying to see who lay or sat on the open wagon bed. "Get out of the way!" the driver shouted. "We're taking them to Doc Smythe." He stood and waved the crowd back, and the mules made slow headway through the gate.

Nathan spotted Arturo's parents struggling to get close to the wagon. He pushed himself toward them and made it through the gate.

Arturo lay stretched out in the middle of the wagon. His head was back. His eyes were closed, and his mouth was open just a little. Other injured miners clutched his hands. Nathan suddenly thought of Harry, the last seconds before he died. Harry's head lay the same way, and on each side Ma and Pa held a hand.

Nathan prayed silently, "Don't let him die, too."

★ SIXTEEN ★

*N*athan stiffened his back and plunged in among all the people trying to reach the tail end of the wagon. He was knocked to his knees in the mud but pulled himself up. Families who didn't find their men on the wagon suddenly turned and streamed back through the open mine gates.

"Are the rest trapped?" Nathan asked. No one answered him. He stayed in place, letting the women and children go past. He spied Mr. Tozzi limping back through the gates. He looked as dazed as if he'd been in the accident himself. Nathan scanned the yard—Ernesto was nowhere in sight. Poor Mr. Tozzi, Nathan thought, he's afraid he's lost them both.

Nathan spun and charged after the slow-moving wagon. Mrs. Tozzi was struggling to climb onto the wagon bed. Nathan pushed forward to boost her, and a man in the wagon offered his hand. She clambered up. She settled herself beside Arturo, put his head on her lap, and stroked his face. From what Nathan could see, Arturo didn't stir.

Mrs. Tozzi pulled off the black scarf that was wrapped about her head and used it to wipe soot from Arturo's face. She had dark red hair that was braided into a bun. Nathan tried not to stare— when he'd seen her before, she had worn a scarf. He had thought her hair was black, like Arturo's. Nathan gazed about. One old man had blue eyes. A baby girl had blond hair. Had he learned anything about Italians? He wasn't sure he'd ever looked closely at any of them.

The mules and wagon plodded up Main Street. People gawked from store porches. Nathan kept in step with the people behind the wagon. The mules turned up the little grade toward Doc Smythe's house. The wagon inched forward. The air hung hot and still. He could see the mules' muscles straining and the sweat beneath the harness. "Come on," Nathan urged.

Beside him two women sobbed. The faces all around him were grim. This was like the procession that had taken Harry to the burying place. Nathan breathed hard. "Wake up, Arturo."

The wagon creaked on. Nathan knew Doc Smythe had just a small office in his house, with a small room for surgery. People sprinted ahead for help, and Nathan saw Mrs. Diggs hobble out of Doc's door. She delivered babies, and the farm wives whispered she wasn't much good at it. What could she do for the injured miners? They might as well have let them lie in the muddy yard. "Where's Doc Smythe?" Nathan called. His own words surprised him—Ma would declare he was being rude.

"White Valley," Mrs. Diggs snapped. "Tending to some young'un that got trampled by a horse." She rolled up the sleeves on her blouse. "Get those bleeding in here first," she ordered the crowd.

At least her straggly hair was tied by a white rag and her clothes were laundered and her face and hands clean. She was better than no one, Nathan supposed. He went to her and tried to sound polite. "Mrs. Diggs, there's a boy in the wagon. He's a friend. He's not moving. Please, come see."

She turned and said, "Nathan, bring him to me. I got others not moving, and some barely breathing." He saw a man with a bleeding gash across his scalp and another with a dangling arm.

Mrs. Tozzi had propped Arturo up against her. Nathan hustled to help. She managed to get Arturo's legs off the wagon, but he was still limp. His eyes suddenly flickered open. His body twitched. Mrs. Tozzi and Nathan steadied him so he wouldn't fall.

Arturo suddenly began wheezing and coughing. His mother wiped his nose and mouth with a handkerchief. Nathan saw the black stains when she took it away. Arturo choked once and then vomited. Nathan stayed with him while Arturo flailed about trying to catch his breath. Trying not to gag, Nathan whispered, "Come on! You're going to make it."

Arturo kept coughing, but he looked at Nathan. Nathan saw his surprise. "I told you that I was going to stay with you," he said.

Nathan leaned Arturo against his shoulder while he gave Mrs. Tozzi a hand down. Between them they half-carried Arturo into the jammed office. Beyond, in the surgery, the table and two iron-framed beds already had people on them. A couple of men lay sprawled on the floor.

Mrs. Diggs set a basin of water on a table and went from miner to miner with a pile of clean cloths. She ordered family members, "Soap the dirt off these men."

Nathan beckoned to her. She came over and looked at Arturo. His head wobbled from side to side.

"He looks better than some," Mrs. Diggs said. She threw open the door to the hallway into Doc's house. "Lay him there and clean him up." She pointed to the carpet-covered hall floor, and she handed them extra rags on which they could rest Arturo's head.

Once they got Arturo down, Mrs. Tozzi knelt to unlace his boots. Her hands were shaking, so Nathan knelt to help her. Suddenly, Arturo moaned and sat up. "Thank you," he said. "I breathe better sitting." So they propped him against the wall.

Nathan was going to wet a cloth to clean him, but Mrs. Tozzi grabbed his hand. She murmured something in Italian. He could not make out the words, but she kept repeating, "*Per favore.*"

It meant "Please," Nathan realized. She wouldn't release his hand. She seemed beside herself.

Arturo managed to speak. "Momma wants Poppa . . . Ernesto." He started to hack. "Tell Poppa I am all right. Where is Ernesto?"

Nathan nodded at Mrs. Tozzi and squeezed her hand. She looked at him with a face so thankful. He rushed out of the house and down the road.

As Nathan approached the mine yard, Mr. Mueller stepped out of the crowd and grabbed his arm. Nathan could tell Mr. Mueller was all in a dither. "And where are you headed so fast? Your ma and pa were just here worrying about you. I sent them up the hill. Stay with me, and I'll help you find them."

Nathan tried to pull away. "I have a message to give someone. Let go, Mr. Mueller."

Mr. Mueller's eyes went even wider. "A message? You mean for one of them?"

"Yes, please." Nathan squirmed.

"This isn't like you—you always do what you're told. Let these Italians fend for themselves. They have accidents once a week. You stay with me."

Nathan yanked free. Mr. Mueller made a grab for him, but Nathan hightailed it to the mine yard.

"Hey, boy, get back here!" Mr. Mueller called after him.

As Nathan ran across the mine yard he spied Arturo's father leaning with a few other workers against a lumber pile. Ernesto was still nowhere in sight. Nathan stopped when a few of the men beside Mr. Tozzi scowled at him. All this sticking to your own kind, he thought. He took a step forward. Mr. Tozzi gestured him on.

Nathan went to him and blurted out, "Mrs. Tozzi sent me. She wants you to know Arturo's all right. He's in the doctor's house up the hill across Main Street."

Mr. Tozzi's face wrinkled. "Slow. Slow, and then I understand, *si*."

Nathan repeated his message, emphasizing the important words, and Mr. Tozzi nodded. The lines in his face disappeared—he had a face like Arturo's, long and thin with a big forehead and a sharp chin. He patted Nathan's shoulder. "You Nathan, *si?* Arturo's pal?"

"Yes." So maybe Arturo still called him a pal.

Mr. Tozzi stared back at the mine entrance.

"Ernesto?" Nathan asked. "He hasn't come out yet?"

Mr. Tozzi shook his head. He put his good hand on Nathan's shoulder. Nathan let it rest there and waited.

Suddenly, Nathan heard shouts. Mr. Tozzi's hand tightened on his shoulder.

Men, streaked with soot and sweat, ran out of the mine. Nathan heard someone call, "We've reached them!"

Nathan could feel Mr. Tozzi shaking, and he let him lean hard to support himself. He carefully led him through the mud to the entry. He and Mr. Tozzi stared into the black hole. The first men rescued were being carried out on the backs of mules. Then a few, holding each other up, stumbled forward from the shadows.

Mr. Tozzi jumped forward. "Ernesto!" he shouted. Ernesto rushed to him. He and Mr. Tozzi bear-hugged. Mr. Tozzi kissed his son on both cheeks. For a moment Ernesto's stern mouth almost smiled. Mr. Tozzi twisted in the hug to yell to Nathan, "Ernesto! He's safe. We all go now to Arturo. *Grazie,* Nathan."

Nathan started toward them, but Ernesto stared at him. Was he frowning? He was so unpredictable. Nathan stepped away even though Mr. Tozzi held out a hand. "I'll run ahead and tell Arturo and Mrs. Tozzi," Nathan said. He took off out the gate.

But there was Mr. Mueller, blocking his way. He grabbed Nathan's arm and said, "You'll not get away from me this time, Nathan. Neither your pa nor me are too happy about who you have been with. I'll bet your parents are over by the depot looking for you. Everybody's headed there. The manager ordered a train to take the badly injured to Gallatin City."

Nathan was so angry he wanted to spit, but he let himself be dragged along. Maybe he did need to see Pa. Maybe this time Pa would stick by him.

★ SEVENTEEN ★

*N*athan spotted his parents standing near the depot platform. Few grownups but many grubby, barefoot children moved about. Mr. Mueller pushed through the crowd of little kids. He nudged them aside with his legs as if he didn't want to touch them.

He placed Nathan's hand right into Pa's. "Hold on to him tight, David, or he's headed for trouble," Mr. Mueller said. "If you saw who his new pal is, you'd know it, for sure."

"Oh, Mr. Mueller," Ma said, shaking her head and looking at the man hard.

But Pa remained silent, and Nathan watched his face. It was hard to read. Pa blinked as Mr. Mueller talked. "Your boy's in so deep that he's even running messages for them. That's why you couldn't find him."

Some color started into his father's face.

Nathan feared Pa would start agreeing, but instead he said quietly, "I don't know that what my son does is anybody's business but Annie's and mine. Nathan doesn't give me or you or anybody trouble. There's an Italian boy his age around. Nathan calls him a friend."

"Look at them!" Mr. Mueller said, pointing to the little kids standing about. "I know with everybody moving away Nathan needs friends—but not *them*. There aren't too many of us Americans left in this town. We're the original settler stock. We need to stick together. None of them will ever amount to much. They come here because they can't do anything else but work in mines—they'd starve in their own country. It's lucky we give them work . . . but to treat them as more than the lowest—"

As Mr. Mueller talked on, Nathan noticed a little boy standing near Ma, yanking on her skirt. He was asking her for something. She bent down. "You want a drink of water?" Ma said.

"Water," the child repeated with an accent. He pointed across the way to the pump at the front of Riggle's lumberyard. Big Jake stood near the pump looking the other way, toward town. "That man," the boy said. "He won't pump for me."

Pa held up his hand to interrupt Mr. Mueller. "Annie," he said. "Keep the boy with you. Nathan, come with me."

Pa headed toward the pump. Nathan kept in step with him. Mr. Mueller stayed with Ma but watched them closely.

"Nathan," Pa said in a low, steady voice, "I want you to know I don't feel the way Mr. Mueller and some of the others do, though sometimes it must sound like it. Do you understand that?"

Nathan nodded. For a while he hadn't been sure, but Pa'd never disliked anybody—he just worried so about what might go wrong. Pa stepped up to the pump and took the tin cup that hung from it. "Jake, do you mind if my boy and I have some water?"

"Let me help you, David," Mr. Riggle said, and worked the handle of the pump until water gushed into the cup. Pa handed Nathan the cup, and then he himself took a long swallow. "The water's always sweet and cold from this well," Pa said. "Is that the bucket your workers use? May I fill it and borrow it?"

"Sure," Mr. Riggle answered.

Nathan saw Mr. Riggle eyeing them warily as they strolled off, Pa carrying the bucket and Nathan the tin cup.

When they reached Ma, Pa took the cup and filled it for the little boy. "Have a drink, son," Pa told him. When the boy had finished, other children gathered around. As Pa ladled, Ma put her arm in his. Mr. Riggle stood over at the lumberyard with his fists on his hips, gawking. Nathan grinned and nodded at Pa.

"Is this whole town going crazy?" Mr. Mueller demanded. "David, what do you think you're doing?"

Pa fixed him with a glare. "We've got some thirsty children here, so I'm giving them a drink. I guess I draw a line at ill-treating anybody."

Mr. Mueller stomped off to Mr. Riggle, and they both stood talking and gesturing. More of the miners and their families were gathering near the depot, lining up along the track. A locomotive hauling a small wooden boxcar and caboose approached. It huffed to a stop near the platform. The miners' children stayed around Pa.

Ma asked Nathan quietly, "Was Arturo in the mine?"

"Yes, and his brother, too. They're out now, but Arturo got hurt a little. He's at Doc Smythe's. Mr. and Mrs. Tozzi are there with him. They thought I'd be back. May I go? I'm only here because Mr. Mueller dragged me. He told me that you and Pa were upset with me."

Ma touched his face. "Pa and I were just wondering what had happened and where you were—that's all. Mr. Hoople told me this train's been sent to take the seriously injured to the hospital in

Gallatin City. He says a wagon is bringing them here. Wait and see if Arturo comes."

Nathan helped Pa ladle for a while. A heavy blond man in a white shirt and serge pants came out on the steps of the caboose and talked to the miners. Some of them clenched their fists and kicked stones along the tracks.

"That's Carlton Hunt," Pa said. "He's a company manager."

"He's the one who ordered the train," Ma added.

If Arturo was hurt enough to go to the hospital, Nathan wondered, how long would he have to stay?

The miners' voices became loud. Nathan winced—Pa was looking worried again. What were they shouting at the man? Whatever it was, Mr. Hunt's face had turned crimson.

Ma pointed up the road. The mule-drawn wagon carrying the injured was approaching the depot. Nathan edged forward with Ma. Pa trailed behind.

The wagon came to a stop, and the miners lifted six men from the wagon and placed them into the boxcar. Family members climbed into the car with them.

"Arturo isn't there," Nathan said.

"He must be all right," Ma said, squeezing his arm.

Nathan glimpsed a hint of a smile on his father's face.

The miners beside the caboose began to shout again at Mr. Hunt. Nathan now saw Ernesto standing right in their midst. He was such a stick-out—a whole head taller than anyone else. No wonder Ernesto's family always worried about his being caught. He pointed him out to his parents.

He could hear Mr. Hunt yell above the uproar, "I want to keep the mine open. But I warn you, if you stop work, the Pittsburgh owners are threatening to send in troopers. You don't want that, and I don't want that. Just keep the mine open."

The miners shouted him down. Mr. Hunt waved to Mr. Hoople, who was standing on the platform. Mr. Hunt stepped into the caboose, and Mr. Hoople signaled with his lantern to the engineer. Steam and smoke puffed from the engine. The train lurched and began to move. Creaking and shuddering, it rolled forward. Nathan stared at the people in the open boxcar and at Mr. Hunt, who looked out the caboose window.

A man started running beside the train. He leaped up and hit the side of the caboose. "This is not over! We will strike!" he shouted.

Other miners moved toward the rolling caboose. One bumped Pa, and the water spilled over Nathan's boots. A rock hurtled through the air, ricocheted off the caboose, and almost hit Ma. Pa hugged the two of them close, shielding them with his body, as the train sped away. Nathan could hear Pa panting.

Some of the men gave chase up the track. The others stood and stared a moment and then began walking away. Pa straightened and released him and Ma. Suddenly, Ernesto and some other miners, walking angrily off, almost bowled them over. Ernesto looked rumpled and wild-eyed, his face still stained with dirt. Then he recognized Nathan. He went red-faced. "Sorry. Sorry," he said, moving away.

"Your brother," Ma asked, "is he all right?"

"Yes, he will be, I think." Ernesto looked at Nathan. "You help my mother—"

One of the men with him pulled his arm and spoke roughly to him in Italian, glaring at Nathan, Pa, and Ma.

"Today is very bad," Ernesto burst out. "My brother hurt. Many people hurt. The mine owners want coal pillars out. But they want us to pay for extra timbers to hold up the mine roof. Already we pay for our blasting powder, our tools, the oil for our lamps. We cannot eat."

Pa started to say something, but the men hurried Ernesto off. As the miners marched up Main Street, both Mr. Mueller and Mr. Riggle rushed over. Mr. Mueller had Rheena tight by the hand. "What did I tell you—you can't mix with people like these. Sell them what they need at fair prices, but don't act like you care about them. When you do, first thing you know, they get uppity and start making demands."

"Mueller's right," Mr. Riggle said. "Carlton only brought that train to help, and look how they acted. He doesn't want this mine closed with a strike—it'll cost him his job, too."

Nathan could hear the fear, even with the anger, in their loud voices. His head hurt.

Mr. Riggle looked toward his stacks of lumber and got even more worked up. "Who knows what more trouble they'll bring? The Pittsburgh newspaper says the steel mill workers in Homestead are talking a strike, too, and right before Independence Day. What do they care? When the miners tried to strike in Connellsville last year, the company sent in Pinkerton detectives to keep order. There was fighting. Heads got busted. The shops and houses of decent people got damaged in the riots. What do you think of that?"

Pa looked both fretful and mournful again. "I don't know anything about it," he answered. "I have more than enough trouble to handle." He turned to Nathan and Ma. "We'd better be getting home to milk."

Ma nodded. She was trembling.

"Can't we go to Doc Smythe's to see how Arturo is?" Nathan asked.

"You know I need help to milk, Nathan," Pa said. "Besides, you heard Mr. Riggle. It may not be safe."

Ma took Nathan's arm. "Arturo's with his family now. We let you do what you had to today. Now it's time for you to come with us."

Nathan moved with them. Was he just going to be put back in harness to the old routine again? Mr. Mueller walked away with Mr. Riggle. Other men crowded around them, unhappy and agitated. There was swearing and name-calling. Nathan was proud at least that Pa wasn't a hothead.

Pa put his hand on Nathan's shoulder and looked him in the eyes. "The miners have it very hard." He sighed and shook his head. "But I don't think you or Ma or I can do much about it."

Nathan felt the weight of that. Just when he'd gotten free, something awful happened. He knew a strike was just what Arturo feared. And if the coal police came here, there might be rioting. Ernesto would be right in the middle of it all. He would cost Arturo and his family their jobs. They would move away—like everybody else—and Nathan would end up alone, trapped on the farm, wishing the next day, the next year, the next century would never come, because he was just plumb scared.

Changes would keep happening, and he wasn't smart enough to come up with any way to handle them. Maybe no one was.

★ EIGHTEEN ★

The next morning when the rooster crowed, Nathan opened his eyes and saw the first light of dawn gleaming about the window shade. He wasn't going to hide in bed. He raised the shade. The fields stretched away, a rich July green. How could a day that was likely to turn out bad look so fine? The mine whistle would soon call the miners to work—if they weren't going on strike. He hung his nightshirt on the peg and pulled on his overalls and boots. If Ma and Pa were just waking, maybe he could convince them to let him go before milking to see how Arturo was.

As soon as he opened his bedroom door, Nathan smelled baking. Downstairs he could hear Ma and Pa talking. Did they ever get a full night's rest anymore?

Ma was lifting her soft white dinner rolls onto cooling racks when Nathan came down the back steps. Kettles boiled on the stove. His mother's straight back and narrow eyes showed that she was in a no-nonsense mood. Pa sipped his coffee with his head down.

"Why did you get up so early?" Nathan asked them. He was surprised Pa wasn't already in the barn.

"Nathan, tell your Ma that the Tozzis might not want to be bothered with us today," Pa said.

"That poor woman has her hands full," Ma said. "And if there's trouble, she'll appreciate having the help of some good food. Somehow Nathan and I will carry it over to her." She smiled at Nathan. "Right?"

Nathan forced a grin but couldn't help wondering if the Tozzis would want their help. They were so proud—would they think Nathan and his parents were acting a cut above them? He only wanted to see if Arturo was all right. "Maybe after milking I could run to ask if they want a visit," Nathan ventured.

"I don't know, Nathan," Pa started. "If the miners are going to strike, the hollow could be —"

Nathan squared his shoulders. He tried to make his voice sound deep. His words came out slow and even. "Really, I'll be fine. Wasn't I yesterday? And with all this food Ma's cooking . . ."

Ma and Pa exchanged looks. "Well, maybe, if

you go right now, no trouble would be starting," Ma said. "I could help Pa with the milking."

Pa nodded slowly, studying him.

"Yes," Nathan said. "I'll be back soon." Before they could come up with more worries, he ran out the door and up the lane. As he crested the hill and started down toward the hollow, his feet slowed. What if everybody in the hollow was sticking to his own kind today? He remembered the faces of those miners with Ernesto yesterday.

He shook his head hard. He really could be as bad a worrier as Pa. He just had to hope that if something happened, he could get himself through it. He marched onto the plank walk near the first row of shanties. The unpainted wood had weathered, and the rust from the nails had streaked the houses. A girl with an angry look threw scrub water over a railing right in front of him. Nathan kept walking.

Farther up the hollow, a group of men had gathered at the corner where Arturo's house stood. Nathan could pick out Ernesto right in the middle of them. Nathan looked at the angle of the sun. They should already be starting off to work. The mine whistle blew. A few of the miners walked up the road. Ernesto and several others shouted and raised their fists at them.

The men stopped and looked back. They whispered to each other. First one ran back to the group, then the others. They shook hands and clapped each other on the back. Not one headed toward the mine.

The strike was on.

Nathan stopped. Pa was right—there was not a thing he could do. And the miners were so heated up they probably would chase him off.

But he placed one boot in front of the other and went forward. The men didn't move from the planks as he approached. He stepped around them into the mud until he came face to face with Ernesto.

Ernesto looked better than he had yesterday. There was a scrape on one cheek, but he had scrubbed himself clean and had waxed his mustache into curled points. He squared his shoulders and leaned toward Nathan.

Nathan tried to make his voice sound deep, as he had with Ma and Pa. "How's Arturo? I want to see him."

Ernesto pursed his lips and looked him up and down. He glared, but he jerked his thumb toward the house and stepped aside. From him, that felt as good as a handshake. The miners let Nathan pass.

He sprinted up the steps, took a deep breath, and raised his hand to knock. The door flew open. Mrs. Tozzi peered at him. This morning her red hair was again covered by a scarf. She spoke in Italian over her shoulder, and Mr. Tozzi came, his arm still in its sling. "Nathan," he said.

Nathan was relieved to see both of them smiling. "Is Arturo all right?"

Mr. Tozzi guided Nathan inside. In the front room Arturo slept, propped up on a blanket-covered pallet by the open window. His sister, Teresa, sat beside him. Her uncovered hair, as red as her mother's, hung in ringlets about her face. She shifted shyly, and Arturo rubbed his eyes and coughed.

Mrs. Tozzi dipped water from a bowl into a tin cup and held it to his lips. When he saw Nathan, Arturo tried to stand, but his mother pushed him back onto the cot. She spoke rapidly to him in Italian, urging him with her hands to stay down.

Arturo gestured for Nathan and whispered hoarsely to him. "She thinks I'll get the lung disease if I don't rest. I told her if you sit beside me, I will be still."

Teresa moved to a chair in the corner, and Nathan sat on the cot edge. "You have to listen to your mother. You might not get well."

"I'll be all right. I'll lie here. I was not hit in the collapse. I was sent down from my trap to work with Ernesto. Before I got there, the shale fell ahead of me. I was knocked out by the dust. A black cloud came roaring at me. I could not breathe."

Nathan could hear the men arguing outside, their voices ringing sharp in the air. Mr. and Mrs. Tozzi opened the door to peer out. "Ernesto wants the strike," Arturo explained. "He will not listen to Momma."

"What does your father want?" Nathan asked.

Arturo shook his head. "He has not decided. He feels helpless with his bad arm, so he stays inside."

Mrs. Tozzi came and spoke to Arturo. "Momma asks if you will eat with me," Arturo said.

Mr. Tozzi nodded from the door. "You'll eat the polenta?" They stared, waiting for him to answer.

"Yes, thank you," Nathan said. But what had he agreed to eat?

Momma and Teresa brought steaming bowls of what looked to Nathan like yellow cornmeal mush with butter floating in it. Arturo stirred his and took a spoonful. Nathan did the same. It *was* cornmeal mush, only sweeter. Nathan grinned. "This is very good."

Mrs. Tozzi rubbed her hands and smiled at him. He returned the smile. He and Arturo ate quickly. Ma always said a good appetite meant the patient would recover.

When Arturo finished, he lay back. "You have finally come to my house."

Nathan's face flared. How could he let Arturo know he was sorry? He nodded. "I wanted to be here."

Mr. Tozzi smoothed Arturo's hair and then collected the bowls. "Nathan," Mr. Tozzi said, "my son tells me your house is very fine. Ours is not so fine. You must forgive it."

Nathan shrugged. He hadn't even noticed the inside of the house. The front room had been painted a bright yellow and beyond that was a blue kitchen. By the door a staircase climbed to what must be tiny bedrooms. A table and a few wooden chairs, all painted white, stood on the bare floors. Nathan didn't know what to answer. Finally, he blurted the truth. "When my great-great-grandparents moved here, they didn't have anything. They built a two-room shack out of logs. You'll get a house, too, after you're here awhile. Our house has gotten so old it creaks at night."

"Here there's hope for people to get houses," Mr. Tozzi said. "Maybe my sons. Ernesto always wants. That's why he talks up the strike. Nathan, when this strike is settled, you come visit Arturo often."

Suddenly remembering, Nathan turned to Arturo. "Ma wants to come visit you now. She cooked for you and your family. What do you think? Do you want me to get her?"

"Visit me? She cooked for me?" Arturo asked, then spoke in Italian to his parents.

"*Si. Si. Grazie*. Bring her," Mr. Tozzi insisted.

When Nathan went out the door, Ernesto was still talking to the men. Most nodded and clapped, seeming to agree with him. Mrs. Tozzi shook her head, and Mr. Tozzi frowned.

Nathan ran along the lane, his legs pumping hard, his whole body feeling lighter. Arturo loved Ma's cooking. Mr. and Mrs. Tozzi would have to like her. She'd like them, too. He sprinted downhill toward home, racing so fast he felt the warm air against his face.

He headed past the last fence before the yard and house but suddenly stopped dead. Pa and Ma stood in the lane facing a big group of men on horseback, several of whom sported billy clubs. Others held rifles at the ready across their saddles. It looked as though the coal company had sent the troopers to stop the strike before it got started. Nathan counted—there were twenty-five horsemen. And they looked ready to pound over the lane into the hollow.

★ NINETEEN ★

*S*omeone had to warn the miners. But if he took off running, the horsemen would quickly overtake him. Nathan edged forward, studying them. They all looked tough. Their tangled hair straggled loose beneath their hats. Most were unshaved. They hadn't brushed the dirt from their ragged uniforms. They didn't seem at all like real soldiers. Nathan's heart pounded. The rough men whom he had seen on Mueller's porch rode with them.

Nathan saw Pa chewing the inside of his cheek. He looked unsure about what to do. Ma had her hands clenched. Nathan stepped right between Pa and Ma and grabbed their hands. Now they made a kind of fence, for all the good that would do.

The horses pranced in place and tossed their heads. A heavy man who sat on the closest horse asked Pa, "This your boy?"

"Yes," Pa replied. He turned his head to

Nathan. "These men are being sent to the company houses to roust out the miners. They stopped to ask if this was the best way through to the hollow. Seems like nobody from the mine yard came along to direct them." Pa looked again toward the men. "Where's Carlton Hunt? Why isn't he showing you the way?"

The leader, whose chin and tunic were stained with tobacco juice answered, "This is none of your concern, folks. We got our orders wired from the Pittsburgh owners. There's agitators making trouble everywhere. We were sent here from Gallatin City. The company won't allow strikes. This mine's going to deliver its coal. We just need to find the troublemakers and root them out before they start anything. That protects you and the town and the mine from real trouble. Now, we just ride along this lane?"

Ma spoke out. "Must you go to their houses? The miners' wives and children are with them."

Some of the men shifted in their saddles, glancing at each other. "We're just here to do a job," the leader said. He started to rein his horse forward.

Nathan shuddered. What would happen when Ernesto let loose on these troopers the way he did on everyone else? Somehow Nathan had to warn the Tozzis.

Think, Nathan told himself. Then he tightened

his hold on Pa's hand. "Pa, shouldn't the troopers ride Robinson Road into the hollow? It's wider," he said, trying to sound helpful.

Pa turned and raised an eyebrow at Nathan. Ma tugged his hand so nobody saw.

"My boy is right." Pa's voice sounded strong and sure. "This lane's just a footpath up past our meadows. You'd have to walk your horses single file. And there're a lot of low-hanging branches. Robinson Road leads right into the hollow. That's how the company hauled stuff in to build the shanties. You just ride down the lane, then go left along the main road a piece. You'll see the road on the left, some muddy ruts among the trees—can't miss it."

Ma clung to Nathan as the men turned their horses and trotted off down the lane. "How did you think of it?" she whispered.

Nathan shook his head. He was just glad he'd gotten it out. He grinned at Pa—he had gone right along with him.

Pa smirked. "They did ask the 'best' way, not the shortest."

"They're not real soldiers, are they?" Nathan asked.

Pa shook his head. "It looks like the owners hired anybody they could to stop the strike."

Nathan touched his arm. "You helped, Pa, and you don't like the miners."

Pa shrugged and flushed. "No matter how bad I feel about the changes," he said, "I don't want people getting hurt."

"I've got to run and warn them," Nathan said as soon as the last horseman had trailed out of sight. "Arturo's brother is one of the 'troublemakers' who's talking up the strike." Before Pa could object, Nathan pleaded, "Please, Pa."

Ma turned on Pa. "Now, David, think of what's at stake here. . . ."

"Do the pair of you think I'm heartless? I'm going myself!"

"No, I have to," Nathan cried. "They don't trust you."

"Nathan, go get Willie out of the field," Ma said.

Pa grabbed his shoulder. "No, it'll be faster if we go on foot." Pa took off, and Nathan sprinted after him.

"I should come, too," Ma called.

"Stay," Pa called back. "If the troopers drive them out, they'll need help from someplace. You've got to be ready."

The two of them pounded up the lane. Pa hadn't stretched those legs of his in quite a while. Nathan surged ahead. He couldn't wait. He might reach the hollow in time to shout warnings—but how could he convince Ernesto and the others to stop, that the troopers had weapons and meant business?

Sweat was streaming into his eyes when he burst into the hollow and raced along the plank walk. A woman, hanging wash by her house, looked startled as he ran by.

The miners were still gathered in the road. Nathan knew that some saw him coming, but they ignored him. Ernesto still stood in their midst, so big he could be spotted a hundred yards off.

Nathan slowed to a walk to catch his breath. What could he say to convince the miners? He never had a real comeback for anybody. Ernesto was so hot-blooded, so foolish. But he didn't deserve to have the company men bash his head, cost him his job, and drag his whole family down. None of the miners deserved that.

There was no getting around it—Nathan was going to have to face Ernesto, whether he liked it or not.

★ TWENTY ★

$\mathcal{A}$s Nathan walked toward Ernesto, the other miners stepped aside. When he reached him, he grabbed one of Ernesto's hands in both of his own. It was as he expected—rough and strong. He had no doubt it could crush both of his at once. "I need your help," Nathan said.

He kept his eyes fixed on Ernesto's. He had his attention, and he had to keep it. "Troopers are coming here now to stop the strike. They have guns and clubs, so we're all in real danger." He heard Pa running up. Pa then was beside him, but he was panting so hard he couldn't speak. Nathan held up one hand to keep him quiet—one wrong word might send Ernesto on a rampage.

Nathan kept cajoling. "If they find out we warned you, they might hurt us—my ma and pa and me." Ernesto was still listening to him. Nathan saw Mr. and Mrs. Tozzi coming toward them off

their porch. Arturo and Teresa stood in the doorway. "You've got to hide us. We lied to save you."

Nathan heard the intake of breath, the voices
of the miners around him. He felt Ernesto's hand
stiffen and pull back, but he would not let go.
"Hide us somewhere. Please. They're going to hurt
us all."

Nathan suddenly felt a rumble in the ground.
"Listen!" he whispered.

Everyone fell silent. Nathan could hear the
hoofbeats coming from Robinson Road. "You have
to go. Hurry! And hide us," he pleaded with
Ernesto. "*Per favore.*"

Ernesto looked like a baffled calf caught in
front of an approaching train. Nathan pulled him
toward his house. He moved. Suddenly, the rest
of the miners scattered for shelter. They yelled to
the women, who snatched up howling children.
Quickly, Mr. and Mrs. Tozzi and Pa were around
Ernesto and him. They all had a hand on Ernesto.
They pushed and pulled him through the door, past
Arturo and Teresa. Mr. Tozzi pushed Nathan and
Pa inside after his wife.

Nathan saw Mr. Tozzi turn away and go and sit
on the top step. He put his leg up as if he was
lounging in the sun.

Nathan started back to him. "Please, come
inside."

145

"No, Nathan. I will talk. Shut the door. You and your poppa cannot be seen."

Before Nathan could answer, Arturo touched his shoulder and nodded. Together they swung the door shut just as the horsemen rode past the house.

Ernesto started forward, but Nathan blocked his path—if he shot out the door, the game was up. "No! No! *Per favore,*" Nathan said.

Mrs. Tozzi exchanged a look with Nathan. She seemed to know what he was up to. She moved toward Ernesto and folded her hands in front of his face, as if she were praying. Then she edged him back from the door toward the far wall.

Nathan huddled with Arturo and Teresa at the front window. Pa stood in the shadows behind, peering out with them. The horsemen thundered past the house, then turned and rode back. Finally, they spread out before the shanties. Pa whispered, "Mr. Tozzi has a lot of courage."

Nathan nodded.

Five troopers rode up in front of Mr. Tozzi, who lit his pipe as they halted, their horses rearing. Nathan recognized the heavy, tobacco-stained man, the leader, who had talked to them at the farm, and another man, the angry farmer from Mr. Mueller's porch.

"You! Miner," the leader called. "Come down from that porch. Talk to me."

Nathan felt the hair stand up on the back of his neck. The man sounded much rougher than when he'd spoken to Ma and Pa. Arturo closed his eyes, and Teresa whimpered.

Mr. Tozzi didn't budge from the porch step. He blew smoke and then held up his bandaged arm. "I am too hurt to move."

"He's smart," Pa whispered.

Nathan nudged Arturo to shore him up.

"Why aren't you at the mine?" the trooper barked. "Where are the other men?"

Mr. Tozzi shrugged and shook his head. "I ache too much to work today. The rest, maybe they are hurt, too. I don't know."

The leader pointed a club at him. It was two feet long, of turned and polished wood, with a leather strap that hung from the man's wrist. Nathan felt as if he were going to explode out of his skin.

He stirred. If only he could get between the men and Mr. Tozzi. They might not hit a boy, and Mr. Tozzi might escape. Nathan stood, but Pa must have read his mind. Shaking his head, he hissed in Nathan's ear, "You did all you could."

Nathan looked at Ernesto. He stood there with worried eyes, listening. Nathan held himself in check—his flying off the handle would only lead to Ernesto bursting out the door.

Outside, the leader rose in his saddle and shouted, "We're here to round up the men and march them to the mine. There will be no strike. Understand? Anybody who doesn't go peaceable . . . their families are out of these houses now and for good." He gestured with his club for his men to dismount and bring Mr. Tozzi.

Just as two were dismounting, four other men on horseback rode up, fast. They weren't troopers. One wore a straw hat, jacket, jodhpurs, and polished boots. It was Carlton Hunt. He rode right up to the leader. "What do you men think you're doing? I'm mine manager—I'm in charge here." Nathan saw him shove what looked like telegrams into the leader's hand.

Mr. Tozzi stood. "Mr. Hunt," he called. "The miners, they do not want a strike." Mr. Tozzi walked toward him.

Ernesto edged forward. Mrs. Tozzi put her folded hands in front of his face again and muttered some words in Italian.

Arturo murmured to Nathan, "She pleads. She said if Poppa is hurt because he moves, she will never forgive him."

Nathan saw her beckoning, and Arturo pushed him forward. "Tell him." For just a moment, Nathan saw Ernesto as Pete's wild-eyed fox cub—scared, trapped, and dangerous. Nathan said to him, "Ernesto, don't you see? Mr. Hunt's your only hope. Just wait. See what he's going to do."

Ernesto groaned, but he stayed in place.

Arturo's father talked a long time to Mr. Hunt. Nathan could see people peeking out of their doors and windows. Then Mr. Tozzi stretched his good hand up to Mr. Hunt, who shook it. With his chin up, Arturo's father stuck his pipe in his mouth and walked past the troopers. Nathan could see a smile on his lips. The troopers scowled. If Mr. Tozzi could just reach the porch without anything happening . . .

★ TWENTY-ONE ★

*N*athan hid behind the door and opened it.
As Mr. Tozzi started up the steps, Teresa rushed out,
threw herself against him, and led him into the
house.

The troopers remounted. Nathan watched their
leader and Mr. Hunt argue a moment. Mr. Hunt sat
straight in the saddle and kept shaking his head.
The troopers finally rode off down Robinson Road.
Mr. Hunt turned with his men and went back
down the lane toward the McClellands' farm.

Mr. Tozzi hugged Teresa and announced, "Mr.
Hunt said if we go to work Monday, the troopers
will go away. Today and Sunday we may rest to get
well after the accident." He mopped his face with a
handkerchief. Nathan wanted to cheer.

Mr. Tozzi walked over to Ernesto, who looked as
glum as ever. He blurted something in Italian. Mr.
Tozzi answered him, and Mrs. Tozzi pressed her

hands together and put them to her lips, as if giving thanks.

Arturo whispered, "Ernesto asks, 'What have we gained? Will we even be paid for the missed days?' We will not be paid, but Poppa says Mr. Hunt promises to inspect the mine every few days. The miners can use extra timbers to support the mine roof, and we do not have to pay for the timbers."

Nathan watched Ernesto. He could see the disappointment. Ernesto wanted so much—Nathan understood that. But at least today he hadn't lost his job and his family's place to live.

Someone rapped on the door. Nathan's throat tightened. Had some of the troopers slipped back, looking for a fight?

"Shh." He looked to Ernesto and put his finger to his lips.

The knock came again. Mr. Tozzi opened the door. Ma stood on the porch. She held a wicker basket filled with food. She brushed her blouse and skirt off before she let Mr. Tozzi lead her in. She looked out of breath as she eyed Pa. "I just saw Mr. Hunt and his men headed back to the mine yard. He shouted that everything was all right. Are the troopers really gone?"

Nathan and Pa went to her. She continued, "From the kitchen window I saw Mr. Hunt heading up here. I ran out and told him the troopers were ahead of him. He said it was all a mistake and took off, riding like the wind. So he got here in time?"

Nathan hugged her. "He got here in time and sent them packing."

Mr. Tozzi pushed Ernesto toward Ma and Pa. "What do you say to these people, eh? They saved you from a broken head. They saved our jobs. Maybe you learn to change things with talk, not charging like a bull?"

Pa shook Ernesto's hand but pointed to Nathan. "Thank him. It was his idea to send the troopers the long way around, so he'd have time to warn you."

Ernesto scowled, squared his shoulders, and stepped toward Nathan. Nathan edged back toward Arturo on his pallet. Ernesto towered over Nathan. "You need my help, you said. You want me to save you. You tricked me, right? I need to be saved from you." Nathan saw Ernesto's eyes were gleaming. He cuffed Nathan's shoulder.

But it had been more than a trick. For once, he had acted as if Ernesto was a friend's brother. And Ernesto had treated him like his brother's friend. Nathan didn't say anything. He just stuck out his hand.

Ernesto gave him a handshake that hurt. "Now

I got two who make trouble all the time for me."

"Save you, you mean," Arturo said.

Ma stepped to Arturo and took his hand. "I heard you were injured. Right now you look like you're doing pretty well."

Arturo held her hand a moment. Mrs. Tozzi and Teresa came forward, and Nathan introduced Ma. Then Mrs. Tozzi gestured that Arturo should stay in bed.

"You sit with me," Arturo said to Nathan.

Ma showed Mrs. Tozzi the basket, and they bent their heads over the food. Ma handed Teresa parcels to unwrap. Mr. Tozzi had cornered Ernesto again and was talking to him.

Pa looked on. Nathan was proud of him—he seemed concerned with problems other than his own. Pa said, "Ernesto, it'll be all right. Carlton Hunt gave his word."

Ernesto shook his head. "It will be all right only for now. The trouble always comes back for us."

Nathan sensed that Ernesto was right. Ernesto would probably be in the middle of it all, and they would have to try to save him again. Pa, Mr. Tozzi, and Ernesto continued to talk.

"You got them together, Nathan," Arturo said, looking around the room.

"My family was easy. I don't know about some

of the other people." They wouldn't give in easily, Nathan knew. The coal mine coming to town had made life better for some, but certainly not for all the farmers or the miners.

"Tomorrow is Sunday," Arturo said. "Maybe I will come to your house and win at mumblety-peg."

"No, I'll come here. Your ma wants you in bed. I have a special collection I want to show you. Remember that box I brought to the pond when . . ."

Arturo made a face. "I haven't forgotten that day."

"Come on. Didn't I follow you far enough to prove I was sorry?" Nathan gave him a you-know-what-I-mean look. Then he got serious. "And I promise always to call you Arturo, all right?"

Arturo grinned. "When you plead with Ernesto, I heard you say 'please' in Italian."

"*Per favore*," Nathan said.

"I'll teach you other Italian words. Can you say '*amici*'?"

"What's that mean?" Nathan asked.

"Friends," Arturo answered.

"*Amici*," Nathan repeated.

"We'll work on it, right, farmer boy?"

"You can bet on that," Nathan answered with confidence. He felt sure of himself. He had convinced everybody, Pa and Ma and the Tozzis, that he had gumption—enough to get himself through most troubles. And, maybe even better, he had convinced himself.

★ ★ ★

FOR MORE INFORMATION ABOUT COAL MINING:

Bartoletti, Susan Campbell. *Growing Up in Coal Country.*
Boston: Houghton Mifflin, 1996.

Freedman, Russell. *Kids at Work: Lewis Hine and the Crusade
Against Child Labor.* New York: Clarion Books, 1998.

Smith, Helene. *Export: A Patch of Tapestry Out of Coal
Country America.* Greensburg, Pennsylvania:
MacDonald-Sward, 1986.

West, Jean M. *Child Labor in America.* Peterborough,
New Hampshire: Cobblestone, 1996.

http://theoldminer.virtualave.net/index1.html

★ ★ ★